In the Future Perfect

BY WALTER ABISH

Alphabetical Africa (novel)

Duel Site (poems)

How German Is It (novel)

In the Future Perfect (fictions)

Minds Meet (fictions)

WALTER ABISH
In the Future Perfect

A NEW DIRECTIONS BOOK

ACKNOWLEDGMENTS
Grateful acknowledgment is made to the editors and publishers of books and
magazines in which some of the material in this volume originally appeared:
*Fiction, Fiction International, New Directions in Prose and Poetry, State-
ments 2*, and *Transatlantic Review.*

The first epigraph on page viii, from Jean-Luc Godard's film *Masculine/
Feminine* (Copyright © 1969 by Grove Press, Inc.), is reprinted by per-
mission of Grove Press, Inc. The second epigraph is from Renée Epstein's
"A Conversation with Alain Tanner" (Copyright © 1976 by Soho Weekly
News), which appeared in the *Soho Weekly News* of November 4, 1976,
and is here reprinted with permission.

The epigraphic quotation on page 1, taken from "The New Spirit" included
in *Three Poems* by John Ashbery (Copyright © 1970, 1971, 1972 by John
Ashbery), is reprinted by permission of the Viking Press, Inc.

Manufactured in the United States of America
First published clothbound and as New Directions Paperbook 440 in 1977
Published simultaneously in Canada by George J. McLeod, Ltd., Toronto

Library of Congress Cataloging in Publication Data

Abish, Walter.
    In the future perfect.
    (A New Directions Book)
    I. Title.
PZ4.A144I   [PS3551.B5]   813'.5'4   77–9443
ISBN 0–8112–0659–9
ISBN 0–8112–0660–2 pbk.

New Directions Books are published for James Laughlin
by New Directions Publishing Corporation,
80 Eighth Avenue, New York 10011

SECOND PRINTING

To James Laughlin

Madeleine: What is the center of the world for you?
Paul: The center of the world!
Madeleine: Yes.
Paul: It's funny. I mean, we've never spoken to each other and
the first time we talk, you ask me such surprising questions.
—*Masculine/Feminine,* a film by JEAN-LUC GODARD

My country has escaped history for a very long time.
—ALAIN TANNER

CONTENTS

The English Garden   1

Parting Shot   22

Ardor / Awe / Atrocity   42

Read-only Memory   58

Access   65

In So Many Words   74

Crossing the Great Void   98

THE ENGLISH GARDEN

> Remnants of the old atrocity subsist, but they are converted into ingenious shifts in scenery, a sort of "English Garden" effect, to give the required air of naturalness, pathos and hope.—John Ashbery, Three Poems

One page in the coloring book I bought showed details of the new airport, the octagonal glass terminal building to the left, and a Lufthansa plane coming in for a landing in the background. It is a German coloring book and the faces accordingly are coloring book faces, jolly faces, smiling and happy faces. By no means are they characteristically German faces. Nothing is intrinsically German, I suppose, until it receives its color.

It could be said that the coloring book accurately depicts almost everything that could be said to exist in the mind of a child, and thousands of children each day gravely apply a color to each face, to each item, to everything that fills a space on the pages of the coloring book in much the same way that it occupies, visually at least, a space in real life.

When one is in Germany and one happens not to be German one is confronted with the problem of determining the relevancy and to a certain extent the lifelikeness of everything one encounters. The question one keeps asking oneself is: How German is it? And, is this the true color of Germany? Looking at the sky one is almost prepared to believe that this is the same sky that the Germans kept watching anxiously in 1923 and 1933 and 1943, that is, when they were not distracted by the color of something else. Something more distracting, perhaps. Now the sky is blue. In German the word is *Blau*. But there are numerous gradations of blue . . . numerous choices for every child . . . The French say *bleu,* and we say *blue.*

The box of crayons I bought is also made in Germany. They resemble the crayons that are made in America, in France, and in Japan. The man waiting for me at the airport could easily have been any one of half a dozen happy-looking individuals on the second, third, and fourth pages of the coloring book. A trench coat slung over one arm. The shoes shined. He had spotted me at once. Speaking a halting but correct English he greeted me warmly. He smiled, hand extended. I touched a smooth dry palm.

The man who came to meet me doesn't drive the car. He sits at my side speaking about his recent trip to Belgrade . . . occasionally he interrupts himself to point to some distant object on the landscape. I obligingly turn my head to look in the direction he is pointing. He wears a well-cut brown pin-striped suit. A sedate businessman's suit. The chauffeur up front wears a uniform. It is a deep green. A forest green. The color of the Black Forest? The sky is overcast. The Mercedes is a dark brown. It is a German vehicle, superb, reliable, and safe. That is not to say that there are no road accidents. Anything can happen on the road. A flat tire, a driver's miscalculation. But these occurrences are not kept hidden from the general public, on the contrary . . .

In the coloring book there are also illustrations of highways that resemble this one almost in every single detail. Nothing has been left out. There it is, the wide asphalt-covered highway that enables the automobiles and the trucks to cover a great distance at a fast clip. We are doing seventy. All around us other cars, Audis, BMWs, VWs and Mercedeses, are heading in the same direction, into the sun. Many of the cars contain families on their way home from a Sunday outing . . . faces colored various shades of satisfied red. Cheerful faces, massive faces, glum faces . . . It is late afternoon. They've had their walk. Their leisurely cup of coffee. They've taken a few breaths of the country air. *Fabelhaft. Hervorragend.* It was worth every minute of the drive. Definitely. It paid off. Definitely.

Everyone I speak to points out that living in Brumholdstein is so convenient. One is, in a manner of speaking, living in the country with all the conveniences that only a city can provide. And only twenty minutes away by car is the country. Only twenty minutes away and one can see cows and horses, brooks, farmhouses, barns, pastures, and people from another century. It'll take them, whoever they may be, at least another twenty years of building to wipe out the country . . .

The German signs on the grass, on the streets, on the highways, at rest stops are there to alert the traveler, just as in the coloring book the same signs are replicated to alert the child of the life that will soon engulf it. Yes, page after page of everything the child can ever hope to see. Tranquil domestic scenes, picturesque landscapes, Papa, Mama, and little Rudi hand in hand strolling in the woods, boarding a Lufthansa plane, visiting the zoo, rowing on a lake, serenity, ah, nature . . . eating at a restaurant, visiting a sausage factory, and joining the modern German army. How exciting, a landscape filled with quaint little stores, gasoline stations, hotels, bookstores, and railroad stations. Here and there a short stout man lifts a stein of beer. The country, according to the coloring book, is once again bursting with activity, a deep compressed energy that on every page displays a space for the color that will become its driving force.

It occurs to me that several pages of the coloring book could easily have been intended to depict parts of Brumholdstein where I am staying. With a few minor alterations it could quite easily become Brumholdstein. And why not. Perhaps the designers of the coloring book had Brumholdstein in mind when they designed the book. Brumholdstein named after the greatest living German philosopher, Brumhold. Somewhere in the coloring book his replica can be seen lecturing to a class. Written on the blackboard behind him are the words: What are we doing today? The philosophical implications of this sentence may be lost on the students, who are only eight or nine years old at the most. This in turn would make it unlikely that the elderly man behind the lectern is Brumhold. Nevertheless, by focusing on the professor and excluding the rest of the class, one can almost hear Brumhold speaking in his quiet controlled low voice, a voice that is also capable of expressing deeply felt emotion, for instance when Brumhold speaks of the many many Germans who, following the First World War, seem to have in the confusing process of what we call history lost their

3

homeland, or at least a section or slice of it. A process, it might be added, that was repeated after the Second World War. The professor could be Brumhold, but he isn't. Brumhold retired years ago. By now he's an old man. He no longer lectures to young Germans. He spends his days thinking and writing . . . writing about why humans think, or fail to think, or try to think, or flee from thought, thereby compelling everyone who reads or tries to read his rather difficult books to think about whether or not they are really thinking or just pretending to think.

Brumhold is not the reason why I am in Germany, but his provocative questions may have been, without my being aware of it, an additional inducement to visit the country where Brumhold's metaphysical questions first saw the light of day. After all, can one, to quote Brumhold, divorce the pleasure of being alive, of traveling in a foreign country, experiencing new sensations, from the very process of meditative thinking. Brumhold writes of the profound need and urge to *think*, and in a sense one must acknowledge that the Germans have always had a penchant for meditative thinking, a form of thinking that may sometimes have verged on brooding. The language they speak has helped them immeasurably to shape their questions, and also enabled them to ask: What is this thinking all about? A question that did not hamper them from successfully building roads and new cities, cars and typewriters, both within the present boundaries of Germany as well as beyond those boundaries.

Still, metaphysics aside, Germans are a pleasure-loving people. They are the first to admit it. They have a word for pleasure, a word for bliss, a word for gratification, a word for rapture, and a word for ecstasy. They also, like the Americans, have a deep and abiding belief in perfection. The perfection of a well-built table, for instance, or a comfortable armchair, or a well-designed city, an attractive park with picnic tables and large shade trees, or a powerful motorcar engine, a formica-topped counter, or the white enamel coating of a pot.

One can see, from examining the people depicted in the coloring book, that all they need is a bit of color to come to life and embrace each other, and then, in the best of humor, stroll over to a nearby café and have a *Bratwurst* or some other kind of *Wurst*, and then, to top it off, see a good film, a satisfying film shot in bright color, the bright color

4

of Germany around them, the color that still remains to be added to these pages, the color that in the film isolates details, the details whose sum is perfection . . . a thought-provoking perfection . . .

Brumhold likes to draw a distinction between calculative and meditative thinking. Fortunately, as far as a child is concerned, nothing that is depicted in the coloring book will force them to think in either one or the other manner. Whoever fills in the color can indulge in a little bit of both.

I love meditative thinkers, said Ingeborg Platt.

Naturally, insofar as any thinking is involved in a technological society, the preference by far is for calculative thinking. It determines the rate of growth in a city, the time it will take to install a pane of glass, break into a bank, paint a mural, compose a twelve-tone symphony, and ask oneself: Who is the stranger on the third floor?

I am the stranger.

What is he doing here?

At present he is contemplatively washing his hands. The soap is German. So are the gleaming faucet and the white basin. The white tiles on the floor and walls are also German, and so are the window frame and the glass and the shower and the bathtub and the view from the bathroom. In the coloring book, it must be pointed out, these details, these objects, these *things* are merely outlines. A child will see the outlines of the bathroom with eyes that can still accept the universality of all bathrooms.

In the coloring book, people, everyday sort of people, go about their everyday sort of life, absent-mindedly washing their hands, brushing their hair, eating their lunch, driving a car, trimming an occasional hedge, the coloring book functioning as an indicator and recorder of all things that are possible. But it is the possible that will never arouse anyone's disapproval. The coloring book simply activates the desire of most people to color something that is devoid of color. In this particular instant it is the normal everyday activity of people in the process of going about their tasks: feeding the dog, the baby, the husband, the

5

tropical fish, themselves, thereby acknowledging a need, not necessarily questioning the need, although they may ponder why . . . why must they feed the tropical fish and the baby and the husband. This in turn leads people to question other things. Why are the workmen at work on another library.

What is the man doing on the third floor?

He is making a local phone call. He is speaking to the Mayor of Brumholdstein. Naturally, the Mayor knows that I am here. He has been expecting my call. He knows where I am staying. He knows the house, the street, and other less pertinent details; for instance, he knows the dimension of the sewage pipe, the width of the balcony, the number of stairs leading to the third floor where I am staying. He has a good head for details. He speaks an excellent English. What's more, he enjoys speaking English. He enjoys saying: You must come over and have dinner with us tomorrow . . . and, I hope you like tropical fish . . . and, Do let me know if there's anything I can do to make you more comfortable . . .

I would have preferred the second floor, but it is occupied, and so is the first. The three-story buildings in Brumholdstein do not have elevators. You'll have a better view than the couple on the second floor, I was told.

Formerly, on this exact location there had been a rather large camp, built along the lines of a city, with a post office, a library, medical facilities, a bakery, offices, tennis courts, recreation areas, trees, all enclosed by several barbed-wire fences. There were German signs all over the camp with arrows pointing in one or another direction. The signs are gone, the camp is gone. It no longer exists. Some of the people in Brumholdstein remember playing in that vast camp, by that time completely run down, windows smashed, telephone wires cut, expensive equipment missing, toilets vandalized. The camp was called Durst. It is not represented in the coloring book. It was built just around the time when Brumhold addressed the student body at the University, attempting to inform them of the plight of their fellow countrymen, Germans who had to leave their homes . . . and the students wept . . . seeing Germans, people like themselves with a bent for meditative thinking, leaving behind what they could not carry with them . . .

6

leaving behind those treasured objects that fall under the philosophical category of: *things*. Tables, chairs, electrical appliances, wood shutters, oak trees, cows, a red barn, a hayfield, all things that in one way or another are reproduced in the coloring book.

Naturally the Durst camp also contained many objects that are to be found on the pages of the coloring book. Benches, chairs, electric light bulbs, kitchen sinks, all now dispersed . . . missing. The familiarity of the objects in the coloring book is reassuring, just as the objects in the Durst camp must have reassured the new arrivals. Ah, look here, a chair, a table. It can't be that bad. And had a coloring book existed of Durst it too would have showed people diligently going about their everyday existence, standing upright, or sitting, or even reclining, chewing food, digesting it, sleeping, walking, all quite normal, speaking before and after breakfast, standing in even rows, saying *Ja* or *Nein* . . . although many, in fact most of the inmates were not German and therefore did not speak a fluent German, which is why most were to some degree incapable in their speech of constructing a proper German sentence . . . and thus were unable to achieve the level of meditative thinking enjoyed by the average well-educated German student.

Brumhold, who in his works has frequently referred to man's flight from thought, has never found the time to visit the city that was named after him. Admittedly, Brumholdstein is only another display of modern architecture, with nicely designed clusters of residential buildings, and shopping centers with arcades, and conveniently located public toilets marked: *Damen* and *Herren*. By ten in the morning the arcade is crowded with shoppers. But no one appears in any rush. People say: *Bitte* and *Danke*. They do not look at each other suspiciously.

They do not look at me suspiciously. Although I am a foreigner. But they are accustomed to foreigners. They feel quite at ease with foreigners. Particularly with foreigners who are familiar with Bach and with Goethe and with Brumhold . . . All one has to do is mention Brumhold and one is accepted, one might even be called a friend. The Germans are quick to use the word. It may have something to do with their heritage, or the old drinking songs which people still sing . . . In the coloring book it is not too difficult to determine who is who's friend

. . . In a sense, everyone depicted in the coloring book is a friend of everyone else.

In 1967 when the first 2,500 apartment units were completed it was decided, on the spur of the moment, that the city should not be named after a statesman, or a poet, or an industrialist, but after a philosopher. Picking the right name was an important event, in part because the city had been built on the site of a former concentration camp. And, in 1967 at least, everyone still felt somewhat disturbed when the subject was raised.

In the great tradition of Greek and German philosophy Brumhold has questioned the meaning, the intrinsic meaning of a *thing* as it manifests itself in the context of metaphysics. There is, moreover, if one stretches the mind a little bit, a certain correlation between a *thing* as we know and understand it to be and 2,500 apartment units, not to mention the additional services, the fire department, post office, library, school, medical facilities, cinema, theater, flower shop, restaurant, coffee shop, bookstore, etc. . . .

Brumhold is by no means a widely read philosopher, but his books are available in Brumholdstein. The Mayor assured me he held Brumhold in great esteem, and so did Wilhelm Aus, the author, whom I visited on my third day in Brumholdstein. Wilhelm Aus being the ostensible reason why I was here.

Knowing something of the history of Brumholdstein, I can only assume that here and there among the population are a number of survivors from the Durst concentration camp. But, for the most part, people here look pretty much alike. Well fed and rather placid. Unless one actually came across a number tattooed on someone's forearm, one could only speculate whether or not the person was a former inmate. Of course, the Germans would be the first to know, the first to recognize a former inmate of Durst.

When Brumhold, like all the men in his age group, was drafted into the militia in 1944, he disconcerted everyone he met by the questions he kept raising regarding the meaning of a *thing* and its correlation to total warfare. If we assume that this is merely a *thing*, he said pointing at his rifle, and this is a *thing*, pointing at his uniform, and each and

8

all of us are doing our *thing*, then our actions, whatever they might be, and whatever they might be called if we were to use the prevailing military terminology, are formulated by our grasp of the *things* around us. Despite the innate grimness of life at that time, Brumhold kept exploring the things he had to do, the things he handled daily in order to implement the things he was ordered to do, although most orders somehow fail to take into consideration the constant narrowing down of certain choices and the elimination of things. Things were being eliminated right and left—in other words, destroyed, put out of action, blown up, erased. Still, as if out of habit, trains kept arriving and departing, trying to meet a certain schedule . . . trying to arrive at a place like Durst, for instance, although each journey entailed a great deal of danger for the men running the train, and the soldiers guarding the train, not to mention the passengers.

The 1940 coloring books are no longer available. They are collector's items by now. Still, indisputably, the things depicted in them are related to the things we find in the latest German coloring book, only the heavy emphasis on the military, on strange salutes, on enthusiastic crowds watching tanks roll by, has been de-emphasized. When Brumhold was drafted into the militia in 1944 there were no coloring books available due to the extreme shortage of paper.

By the time work started on the first 2,500 apartment units, the Durst concentration camp had been almost entirely demolished. In history it took second place to the more notorious camps such as Dachau, Auschwitz, and Treblinka. After giving it some thought, the community decided that the former concentration camp was not worth keeping as a monument. It would not attract a sufficient number of tourists to warrant the extensive repairs that were needed. Furthermore, the camp had only two gas ovens. For the price of rebuilding and maintaining the Durst concentration camp they could build 2,500 apartment units. A lot of kids from the neighboring townships regretted the decision. They used to play soccer and other games on the grounds of the former concentration camp.

The Mayor of Brumholdstein is an affable young man in his thirties. Dark business suit and a polka-dot tie. He introduces me to his wife and to their friend Ingeborg Platt, a librarian at the local library. I'm afraid we don't carry your books, she said to me.

The Mayor lives in a two-story building that is only a few minutes' walk from the city hall. Three bedrooms, two bathrooms, ping-pong in the basement. Care for a game before dinner, he asks me.

Cold cuts are served at dinner somewhat to my surprise. Smoked sausage, potato salad, crisp green salad, cold beer, then cheese and fruit. I mention how much I liked the design of Brumholdstein.

We're entirely self-sufficient, said the Mayor with a smile. Electrical generator, sewer disposal plant, we even make our own street signs.

Do you have a graveyard, I inquire jokingly.

He frowned. No, not a graveyard. Our population is a young one, although we've had a number of deaths, naturally. At present burials take place in one of the two old graveyards situated in the adjacent county.

Do people ever disappear, I asked.

Disappear? He looked astonished.

In America people frequently disappear. A man or woman goes out to buy a pack of cigarettes or a newspaper and is never seen again.

Why? asked his wife.

They're probably desperate, said Ingeborg Platt.

The Mayor examined me somewhat dubiously. I understand that you will be meeting Wilhelm Aus tomorrow. He is one of our best writers. I hope you will enable him to reach a wider audience.

Are you familiar with his work, I asked Ingeborg Platt.

I find him a bit turgid, and heavy on the politics . . . but he can be fascinating.

He's the new spirit, added the Mayor. A bit to the left, but—

Do you know him well?

The Mayor laughed. Quite well. He is married to my younger sister. At first he didn't want to move to Brumholdstein. Too modern . . . too antiseptic . . . He was afraid that it would affect his work. But he'll tell you all about it. I'm afraid he's not very reticent . . .

Incidentally, are there any former inmates of the camp living in Brumholdstein?

The Mayor looked blankly at me. Inmates? He turned to his wife. Are there any inmates of the former camp in Brumholdstein? I think, she said slowly, there may be one or two. I think the projectionist at the local cinema is a former inmate . . . someone told me that he was . . .

Some settled in this area, said the Mayor, and became immensely successful. They had a certain advantage.

Advantage?

Well, in having survived, you know.

There are letter boxes on all the streets as well as public telephones. The telephones are not enclosed, and one's conversation could be overheard.

Crime? The Mayor laughs loudly. He is delighted to be questioned about crime. It is virtually nonexistent. Occasionally the police pick up a vagrant, an out-of-towner. They are conspicuous. From the police point of view, he added carefully, Brumholdstein was an easy town to protect. No little alleys, or empty buildings.

I left at ten together with Ingeborg Platt. She was married for five years to an architect. She now lives on the second floor of a red-brick building that is within walking distance of the library. She wears glasses. She too, as a child, used to play on the former grounds of the Durst concentration camp. I discover that she is an avid reader, attends the local performances of the symphony orchestra, and even plays the cello. Her former husband has remarried and lives in Frankfurt. He's an excellent architect, Ingeborg said almost fiercely. He designed the library I work in. The little groups of residential buildings are arranged in such a way as to insure maximum privacy for the tenants of the buildings.

I doubt that anyone saw her visit my apartment. Like the Mayor, she too was born in the neighboring town of Rinz. A great many of her friends still live there.

Why did you really come to Brumholdstein, she asked me.

This is Germany. The doors and windows are different from the ones in America. But they are solid doors and windows. And the people look healthy, self-satisfied, perhaps a shade smug. Not Ingeborg, she's one of the exceptions.

Where were you in 1942.

11

I wasn't born, answers Ingeborg.

We've just met a few hours ago. We're lying in my bed. Why don't you remove your shirt, she asks. We only know each other for five or six hours. Do take off your shirt, she says. She is naked and crouching on the floor in front of me. Actually, she is not crouching on the bare floor, but on a carpet that was manufactured in Germany. She knows the Mayor and his family, Wilhelm Aus and his family, and the bookseller Sonk who is a bachelor. She sees them all quite frequently. I watch her crouching in front of me. Who else, I wonder, shares this vision of Ingeborg with me?

Ingeborg is attempting to give me pleasure. She is doing it in a completely selfless and unselfconscious manner. It is, admittedly, not an entirely new experience, but the familiarity of the experience is colored by the unfamiliar world around me, a world housing unfamiliar *things*, that the remoteness, the polite distance between Ingeborg and myself serves only to intensify, although what I interpret as distance may merely be due to the way we express or fail to express ourselves in both English and German.

So when she asked: Was that nice? I didn't really know if it was . . . being annoyed by the way the question was phrased, being irritated by the word nice, being reluctant to say yes, not because the experience had not been *nice* but because the word nice had been discarded long ago from my day-to-day vocabulary.

I will have them order all your books at the library, she said later, trying to please me.
    That's nice.

Ingeborg's father had been a colonel in the Waffen SS. I showed her my coloring book and the crayons, surprised by her response. It is a gift for a little boy, I said, forcibly having to restrain her from coloring the pages.

Is your father alive, I asked her cautiously.
    Oh yes, he's just retired.
    From the army?
    Oh no, from a bank . . .

Shortly before she left, she said: Well, another German experience for you . . . and because she was speaking in English, I couldn't determine the degree to which she intended this statement to be an accusation.

The people of Rinz, a neighboring town where Ingeborg grew up, had grave reservations regarding the building of a city so near their town. Brumholdstein, once completed, would attract people from all over Germany. There would be more cars, more roads, more bars, more stores, more single people, more venereal disease, more crime, more fires, more schools, more police, and higher taxes and an end to the tranquility they had enjoyed for so many years . . .

At night I feel somewhat chilly and cover myself with another blanket that had been thoughtfully provided for me. The local German newspaper is delivered to my door. Among other details it also lists the daily TV programs. Glancing at the listing I discover that Wilhelm Aus is to be interviewed the following day at 10 a.m.

I came to Brumholdstein in order to visit Wilhelm Aus. He is expecting me. And quite clearly, to judge from the TV interview, he's an old hand at being interviewed. Born in 1946, he has published three novels and two books of essays. He is referred to as one of the young and upcoming German writers. As a child he played in the Durst concentration camp with his school friends. Although not exactly unaware of the purpose the camp had served during the war, he and his friends in converting sections of the camp to another purpose saw no reason ever to dwell on what may or may not have taken place in the large shower room where they played handball, or on the parade ground where they played soccer . . . Much to Wilhelm's regret, he did not excel at any sport. He did not excel at anything. No one, not even his teachers, had any inkling that he would become an influential writer. Even his parents were surprised. Gradually they came to accept his decision to become a writer, just as they had come to accept his left-wing politics. Mr. Wilhelm Aus cuts his own hair, which is why the local barber looks at me with blank eyes when I mention Aus. *Aus, Aus? Nein, denn kenn ich nicht.*

Ingeborg had asked me if I was married.
    Yes, I said.
    What is she like?

I showed her a photograph I carry in my wallet.

She's attractive . . . what does she do?

She's a psychologist. As a matter of fact, she also happens to be Jewish, and a number of her close relatives were killed in the Durst concentration camp.

Seeing the startled look on Ingeborg's face, I burst out laughing. No . . . no . . . forgive me, I couldn't resist saying that . . .

Saying what? That your wife is a psychologist, that she is Jewish, or that her relatives were killed in Durst.

The last bit about her relatives. I don't know where they were killed. Forgive me, it was a terribly cruel thing to say to you.

I take it that she didn't wish to accompany you to Germany, said Ingeborg.

Not exactly. In a manner of speaking we are separated . . .

Divorced?

No . . . living apart.

I see. She has her life and you have yours.

Did this conversation really take place? Can I rely on my memory? The people in the coloring book go about their daily business, and in doing so they too have to rely on their memory. Anything in the world can trigger a recollection of an event. Ingeborg left her scarf in my apartment. She forgot it. It is a bright-colored silk scarf made in India. It has been left behind to remind me of an event that had taken place in this third-floor apartment.

It goes without saying that a large number of people in Brumholdstein are aware of my presence.

What is he doing in Brumholdstein?

He came to interview Wilhelm Aus.

What is he doing now?

He is watching TV.

What did he do last night?

He made love to Ingeborg Platt.

Why didn't he remove his shirt?

Well, Ingeborg, says Wilhelm. I hear you've gone to bed with our visitor from America.

One can't any longer keep a secret around here, she replies.

He's married, I take it.

Yes . . . but they're separated. He hasn't seen her in some time.
Why did he refuse to take off his shirt?
Because he is hiding something.
What could he be hiding beneath his shirt?

During the TV interview Wilhelm Aus refers to the foreign laborers in
Germany. Our garbage is being hauled away by Turks, Yugoslavs, and
Italians, our streets are being cleaned by Rumanians. These people are
providing us with cheap labor. We are exploiting them.

Wilhelm Aus is married to an attractive blonde schoolteacher. They
have three children. Each year they take their vacation in the Black
Forest where they rent a large cottage. They eat sausage three times
a week. It is my impression that neither Wilhelm or his wife appear
likely to do anything unexpected . . . commit suicide, disappear, or kill
someone . . . It is just an impression. I have been proved incorrect once
before. There are white tiles on the floor of their apartment. The metal
railing on the staircase is black. The stairs like the exterior of the
building are also made of red brick. There are two apartments on each
floor, although now and then a more affluent family occupies an entire floor.

Mr. and Mrs. Wilhelm Aus are not affluent. There are three children
to be fed. In twenty years, provided nothing unexpected takes place,
they may become affluent and occupy the next-door apartment. Naturally, Wilhelm Aus may just strike it lucky with one of his novels one
day. But this seems, given the experimental nature of his work, somewhat unlikely. In the TV interview the likelihood of his occupying the
next-door apartment is not mentioned. It is not controversial enough. It
does not have sufficient public appeal, besides it may alarm his next-
door neighbor.

On my second visit Mr. Aus says, call me Wilhelm. His wife says, call
me Johanna.

Wilhelm Aus accompanies me back to my place. In the evening he
walks his dog. They stop periodically at a street lamp, a post box, a
public telephone, a parked car. Each evening they follow the same
route. Each evening Wilhelm Aus meditatively watches the yellow
stream of his dog's urine stain the sidewalk, or the tire of a German

car. What is Wilhelm thinking as he watches his dog piss? He knows that I have slept with his friend Ingeborg. Both he and his wife know that I have failed to undress completely while making love to their close friend. Why don't you take off your shirt, Ingeborg had asked. I prefer not to, I replied.

The bookstore is on the main street. The owner, Max Sonk, a former student of philosophy, had studied with Brumhold in 1941 and 1942.

On his desk there's a photograph of Brumhold addressing the student body of Mannheim University in 1936. The photograph is inscribed to, My dear Max Sonk. Max Sonk knows who I am, but he is outwardly, at least, indifferent to my presence in his bookstore. He sees Ingeborg at least twice a week. Like me he has been to bed with her.

Mr. Sonk congratulates Wilhelm Aus on the telephone for the way he handled the interview on TV. You were really excellent. I admire your candor.

Have you seen Ingeborg lately, Wilhelm Aus wants to know.

We've had a slight falling out. She'll probably come around in a day or two.

Now the street signs and all the directional signs that are erected on the highway are being manufactured in Brumholdstein. Once they were made in the neighboring town. It goes without saying that the people of Rinz deeply resent this. They also resent that the few foreigners employed by the department of public works in Brumholdstein all live in Rinz. Now we have Turks and Rumanians walking on our streets, is the common complaint. Despite everything that is being said about them, the Italians, Turks, and Yugoslavs are hard workers. The streets of Brumholdstein are clean, the garbage is picked up on time. No complaints there. But no one really wishes to have these people as next-door neighbors. As neighbors they leave a lot to be desired. In no time little grocery stores carrying foreign foods are opening up on every corner in Rinz.

I took Ingeborg to a Chinese restaurant . . .

Why do you dislike me so much, she asked.

Are you quite sure you have the right person, I answered.

In the coloring book there is no evidence of anyone ever showing any dislike for another person or thing. Dislike has been permanently effaced from the world of this coloring book. The faces still awaiting to receive their color show only contentment and pleasure.

Is everything satisfactory? asked the Chinese waiter.

But why did you pick on me? Ingeborg asked.

I don't really understand what you're saying.

At night I feel chilly and get up for another blanket. I am by now accustomed to sleeping alone. After a week in Brumholdstein, I've come to feel at home in this apartment. There's a white telephone at my bedside in case I wish to make a call at night, or receive one. There is another phone in the kitchen, also white, and a third, this one is black, in the living room, just to make sure that I won't miss a call. In the living room on a shelf there are a number of German and English books. Among the German books are two by Brumhold, *Ja oder Nein* and his great classic, *Uber die Bewegung aller Dinge.*

Before going to bed a man takes a shower, brushes his teeth. So far, nothing unusual. Like most people, whatever I do inside the bathroom is done unthinkingly. In a sense, all my needs are being taken care of. They have even provided me with a typewriter. The refrigerator is stocked. More cold cuts and beer.

This city is named after a German philosopher, who, like so many of his predecessors, inquired into the nature of a *thing.* He started his philosophical inquiry by simply asking: *What is a thing?* For most of the inhabitants of Brumholdstein the question does not pose a great problem. They are the first to acknowledge that the hot and cold water taps in the bathroom are things, just as much as the windows in the new shopping center are things. Things pervade every encounter, every action. In that respect, the person who says, I'm doing my thing, may have a sequence of personal events in mind, the self receiving a priority over the things, although the self could never even formulate a conception of its role without them.

Are you married? asked Johanna.

Yes.

You should have brought your wife along.
She was here in Germany a long time ago.
Wilhelm did not ask me when.
What does she do? asked his wife.
She's a psychoanalyst.
How fascinating.
That could be a problem, said Wilhelm slyly.
Not any more, I explained.
They looked inquiringly at me.
Initially it was something of a problem, but not any more . . .

I wash my hands. The desk is uncluttered. I find a ream of paper in one of the drawers. In another drawer there's a German-English dictionary, a bottle of Pelikan fountain pen ink, an eraser, a plastic ruler, and a small stapler.

I look up the German word for missing. It is *abwesend,* or *fehlend,* or *nicht zu finden.* I also look up the word, disappear. It is *verschwinden.*

I telephone Ingeborg wishing to apologize for my rudeness the night before. But no one answers. Finally I leave the apartment. The tobacconist from whom I buy a pack of cigarettes used to live in Berlin. On an impulse I buy a lottery ticket although I don't expect to be in Germany when the winners of the lottery are announced. I ask the young waitress at the small restaurant where I have a late breakfast if she was born in the area. She laughs. Oh yes. Did you also come here to play before they started to build Brumholdstein. Oh yes, we all did. At first the guards who guarded the empty camp used to chase us away . . . but after a while they became less strict about it. The short stout man at the next table is listening to our conversation. He is holding a newspaper in front of him, while eating scrambled eggs, fried potatoes, and sausage . . .

After a careful search that afternoon I found the old railroad tracks. They run parallel to the main highway. There was very little traffic at that hour. I parked my car on the side of the highway and followed the tracks on foot for a mile or so. No one saw me. I encountered no one. In the distance I could make out the taller buildings of Brumholdstein. On a siding I passed an old railroad freight car. Its sliding doors wide open. It was a German freight car. For no reason in particular I scratched a long row of numbers on its side.

Miss Ingeborg Platt failed to show up at the library on Monday morning. She usually arrived at nine-thirty. She would take her one-hour break at twelve. In the past she had always called in when, for one reason or another, she couldn't come to work that day. She liked her job and was exceptionally good at it. For the past two years she had been in charge of cataloging. Although somewhat remote, she was well liked by the staff. She was neat, methodical, accurate, with an excellent memory for the titles and names of authors of the books she catalogued, and the dates of their arrival at the library. It so happened that she also was an avid reader, quite eclectic in her taste, reading anything that stimulated her imagination. She was able to borrow books before they were put into circulation. That has long been one of the few privileges librarians possess. Although well liked she had few friends.

Was she really well liked, I asked Wilhelm, after she had been missing for a few days. No, she was not. She kept herself apart from the others. I think she was afraid of being rejected. She was also afraid that they might find out that her father had been the former commander of the Durst concentration camp, although, I should think, that is common knowledge by now.

She told me that the last time I saw her, I admitted.
And?
And nothing.

When she failed to show up at work, the chief librarian, a Mr. Runz, concerned that she might not be feeling well, telephoned her several times during the day. Receiving no reply, he drove over to where she lived at around five-thirty. After trying her doorbell a number of times, he went to see the superintendent, a Mr. Kurtz, who was most reluctant to become involved. Only after a great deal of persuasion did Mr. Kurtz open her apartment door. The place was empty. Nothing seemed to be missing. It was Mr. Kurtz who noticed that the electric plug of the refrigerator had been pulled out of the socket in the wall.

The refrigerator was stocked with food, cold cuts, vegetables, meat, milk, butter, beer . . .

Wilhelm rang me late at night to tell me that Ingeborg was missing. He called to inquire if by any chance I had seen her that day. I suppose it was a tactful way of trying to discover if she was staying with me.

I haven't seen her since last Thursday. We had dinner together at the Chinese restaurant. She seemed quite cheerful at the time.

What did she wear?

An ivory-colored dress with gold buttons.

I'll come to see you tomorrow, said Wilhelm. He sounded cold and stiff.

This being Germany, a nation known for its thoroughness, I expected to be questioned by the police. But they never got in touch with me. The Mayor called me the next day and awkwardly made up some excuse as to why he couldn't see me at his home that evening. I never called him to say good-by.

I did not object when Wilhelm came by to take me to Ingeborg's apartment. He simply said I might help him determine if something was missing. I had spent two nights and several evenings at her place and by now was quite familiar with the layout. I could see it with my eyes shut. It was clearly imprinted on my mind. White walls. A bedroom, a living room, a small kitchen. Room enough for one or two people, and their objects, their things. There were plants, a stereo, books, a few drawings on the wall. Her suitcases were in one of the two built-in closets. The ivory-colored dress was hanging in the other closet. There were no notes. Her check book, bank book, and other personal papers were in a drawer of her desk. Wilhelm came across the coloring book I had given her. He did not object when I took it with me. He didn't seem to care very much about it. I also pocketed the crayons.

Wilhelm told me that he had been in touch with her former husband.

What about her parents?

They haven't been on speaking terms for years.

Why did she disappear, I asked.

Evidently something must have happened, said Wilhelm grimly.

Whatever it was, it could have been troubling her for a long time. Yes, Wilhelm agreed. But it also could have happened just now. She'll be back, I said without much conviction. I doubt it, replied Wilhelm.

Going through her desk drawers I came across a photo of a group of skeleton-like men standing in a row, posing for the photographer. Wilhelm studied the photograph, the building in the rear was one of the buildings in the former Durst concentration camp. The men were smiling incongruously. They were leaning against each other for support. Under a magnifying glass I could clearly make out the numbers tattooed on their forearms.

This photo must have been taken a day or two after the camp was liberated by the Americans, said Wilhelm. I made absolutely no move to stop him as he carefully and deliberately tore the photo into tiny shreds. I did not lift a hand to stop him from effacing the past.

When I left Brumholdstein, no one saw me off.

I had a cup of coffee at the airport snack bar. The short stocky man at the next table raised a stein of beer. *Prost,* I said. Just before take-off, I tossed the coloring book and the crayons into a garbage can. The man who stamped my passport said: Come back soon.

Auf wiedersehen.

PARTING SHOT

1

I returned from Morocco in September in time for my exhibition of photographs at the Light Gallery on Madison Avenue. Most of the exhibition was devoted to photographs I had taken of the Mosque of Kairouan and of the city of Kairouan which is surrounded on all sides by an arid plain. At the very last moment, before the exhibition was to open, I decided to include a photograph I had taken of Irma on a West Side pier a week or two before my departure for North Africa. I was fully aware that the photograph was out of context with the exhibition and might even be disconcerting to a viewer looking at the Great Mosque and the innumerable shots I had taken of the shrouded women in Kairouan. I included the photograph of Irma for no particular reason that I can understand. I had invited her to accompany me to Morocco and Tunisia, but she couldn't make up her mind, and I finally left without her. I worked in my darkroom on the print of Irma in her one-piece bathing suit only after my return from North Africa. At the opening the gallery was packed with people, and in general the show was well received. I sold about a dozen prints the first night. In all I sold eight prints of the photograph of Irma sunning herself on a bench at one hundred and twenty-five dollars each, but of the eight buyers only Gregory Brinn called to invite me to his place on Central Park West for a drink. I remember looking everywhere for Irma at the opening, but apparently she never made it.

A friend of mine informed me that Gregory Brinn was an authority on Guy de Maupassant, who incidentally had visited and admired the

Great Mosque of Kairouan in 1889. Brinn was also a literary critic, and his wife was the daughter of Emmanuel F. Hugo, a well-known and extremely popular writer. Somehow, I had not expected to be the only guest invited that afternoon; however, both Gregory Brinn and his wife, Maude, were extremely cordial. Somewhat furtively I looked around for the photograph he had bought and finally located it on a bookshelf in his study. The photograph was inside a Kulicke frame.

From his desk Gregory Brinn had a superb view of Central Park eighteen floors below and, whenever he chose to turn his head slightly to the left, a view of Irma in her one-piece bathing suit. I must admit I was somewhat disappointed that he had not picked one of the photographs of the Great Mosque. As an authority on Maupassant who had written with great eloquence of the latter's visit to the Mosque, Brinn's failure to choose one of the Kairouan photographs struck me as odd. She has a striking face, he said, referring to Irma. He then asked me if I was attracted to the kind of cold sensuality Irma exuded. I couldn't think of an appropriate answer.

What makes you decide to photograph someone, Gregory asked me just before I left. I walked out of their apartment with a vague sense of having been used. I felt that I had been asked over in order to supply Gregory Brinn with information regarding the woman in the photograph he had bought. Perhaps he felt that for the price he had paid I should provide the information. When I had said that I knew Irma quite well, he had promptly asked me if I ever had an affair with someone simply as a result of having taken their photograph. Well, Irma is always photographically available, I replied, expecting him to laugh. With no change of expression on his face, he stared at me, apparently trying to evaluate what I had said.

The following day his wife went to the gallery and bought one of the photographs of the Great Mosque, one that had two men in white cloaks standing in the background. She paid with her own personal check. I think she bought the print purely as a way of apologizing for her husband's behavior. I had been invited over on a false pretense, and she knew it. My first impulse was to ring her up and thank her for buying the print, but I then realized how awkward and stilted the conversation would be, since her purchase had only been a gesture, whereas I, as a professional photographer would be thanking her for her supposed good taste, and her admiration for my work.

Months later I ran into her on Madison Avenue. She was looking at a blue blazer on display in one of the shop windows at Tripler's. Do you like it, she asked anxiously, momentarily leaving me with the impression that she intended to buy it for me. It's very handsome, I said. I'm so glad you like it. I intend to get it for Gregory. He looks so good in a blazer. I could tell that she was very much in love with him.

By the way, what's the name of the woman in the photograph you took?

Irma, I said reluctantly, Irma Dashgold.

She's awfully attractive. I believe Gregory's fallen in love with her. Do you see her often.

Now and then.

You must come and see us again, she said politely. Gregory and I enjoyed your visit immensely. I wanted to thank her for buying the print of the Great Mosque, but didn't.

I fell in love with Irma the first time I saw her. I was much younger, and it was easy to fall in love with her, or perhaps I should correct that and say that she made it easy for one by treating love the way she treated everything else, with a kind of elegant casualness.

What does she do? Maude asked.

Who?

Irma.

I really don't know.

She said good-by and then entered Tripler's, I assume to buy the blazer. I hoped I would not run into her again, since the encounter had made me remember her gesture. It also reminded me of her husband and their very beautiful apartment on the eighteenth floor. I remembered the view from the apartment, as well as the gleaming parquet floor, and the way each object in the apartment appeared to have been carefully placed where it was in order not to detract from the beauty of another object. Visiting their place was a little bit like going to a museum. Although Gregory Brinn was successful, it was mostly if not entirely her money, or more precisely, her father's money that had paid for everything in the apartment. I could not efface the photograph of Irma sitting on his bookshelf within close proximity of his desk. It may have been the reason why I never displayed Irma's photograph in my place, although I was greatly tempted to.

2

The large plate-glass windows of the stores on Madison Avenue are there to protect the intrinsic value of the plaid suit, of the hound's tooth hunting jacket, of the blue blazer, the purple polo shirt, the polka-dot scarf, and what are essentially tastefully arranged objects in the shopwindow, without for a second depriving the passerby of the perfection of the merchandise.

Does the accumulation of what is perfect indicate wealth. The large plate-glass windows are always clean. They not only permit a viewer to see what is inside the shopwindow, they also reflect what stands and moves outside the store. It is not entirely uncommon to see a man wearing a blue blazer stop to look at what appears to be the exact replica of his jacket in a shopwindow. It is, in fact, wealth that permits the easy replication of what is perfect, despite Whitehead's admonition: *Even perfection will not bear the tedium of indefinite repetition.*

Did Whitehead know that wealth enables people to acquire the perfect apartment, the perfect country house, the perfect haircut, the perfect English suits, the perfect leather and chrome armchair, the perfect shower curtain, the perfect tiles for the kitchen floor, and a perfect quiche available only from a small French bakery near Madison Avenue, and the perfect Italian boots that look like English boots but are more elegant, and the perfect mate, and the perfect stereo, and the perfect books that have received or undoubtedly are just about to receive a glowing review in the *Saturday Review.* Wealth makes it so much easier to have the perfect encounter with a stranger, enjoy the perfect afternoon, make perfect love, a sexual encounter that is enhanced by the objects that are in the room, objects that may at one time have attracted a good deal of attention while on display in a Madison Avenue shopwindow.

I do not feel well, said Maude. I distrust Gregory with all my heart. I also distrust my own acquisitiveness, and my occasional generosity.

Why on earth did I buy Gregory that two-hundred-dollar jacket. What I really would like is to spend my life somewhere in the country, away from the stores. I would like to stroll down a country lane, surrounded by horses and whitewashed barns, and wave to friendly yet aloof farmers with weatherbeaten faces. I do not feel that the perfection of anything in this apartment has enriched my life in the slightest. All it has done is to protect me from what I consider garish and crude. I walk around in the nude to combat the incipient coldness of Gregory. How easy it is to give in to his remoteness and to surrender and embrace his sexual indifference . . . We no longer make love. We occasionally fuck . . . two collectors of the perfect experience, assessing the degree to which we have arrived at the state of perfection.

3

Gregory does not know where in the city I had taken the photograph of Irma. It will take him some time to find the pier with the double row of benches on either side. People who visit the pier walk up one side and then return by the other. When I took the photograph early in the morning most of the benches were not occupied. I let Irma pick one. What do you want me to do. Anything you like, I said. She was wearing her one-piece bathing suit. Her feet resting on the bench in front of her, she leaned back and shut her eyes. She was posing, she was also trying to decide whether or not to accompany me to North Africa.

Everyone who enters Gregory's study comments on the photograph.
Isn't that a Kulicke frame?
Yeah.
Who is she.
I saw the photograph at a gallery on Madison. She possesses a certain almost undefinable sensual coldness that I find attractive.
They stare at Irma. Their eyes dissect her. I see what you mean.

I wonder what she does, Maude remarked to Gregory.
Why don't you ask the photographer.
She smiled. I will, the next time I see him.
Why don't you give him a ring. He's in the book.

4

Don't you think you ought to put on a robe instead of parading naked around the house, said Gregory. There are people out there. Gregory pointed at the houses on the other side of the park. You may not know it. It may not occur to you, but anyone looking into our apartment must get a curious impression of the way we live.

We're on the eighteenth floor, she reminded him.

I still wish you wouldn't walk around in the nude.

I wonder if you have the vaguest idea of how irritating you are, said Maude.

I merely suggested that you put on a robe. People talk. The doorman has been giving me the strangest looks for the past month.

People talk. Is that what you would say to that glorious beauty in your study. You'd be off like a shot if you had the teeniest chance of fucking her.

Oh well, said Gregory, I better take a walk. I don't want to stand in the way of one of your little melodramas.

From their apartment on the eighteenth floor Maude can see the buildings on Fifth Avenue across the park. Using Gregory's binoculars, she can make out Gregory's tall figure in his blue blazer as he heads for the other side of the park, turning occasionally to look at someone who has attracted his attention. Once he turned around, as if sensing that he was being observed, and, shading his eyes against the sun with one hand, stared at their building, at their floor, at her standing naked at the window. But at that distance she could not make out the expression on his face. There really was no need to see his expression. It never changed. He was going over to Madison to look at the latest exhibition of photographs at the Light Gallery.

5

Maude called her closest and dearest friend Muriel. Tell me, she asked impulsively. Have you and Gregory ever fucked. I won't be mad if you say yes.

Do you take me for some kind of shit, said Muriel. I don't screw around with married men if I happen to know their wives.

Then what about Bob?

But that's different. I can't stand Cynthia. Look, why don't you come over and talk about it.

What's there to talk.

Whatever's on your mind. Whatever made you pick up your phone.

I can't make it today, said Maude firmly. Maybe tomorrow.

Not before eleven, said Muriel.

Do you ever sunbathe on a park bench.

Never, said Muriel emphatically. I can't bear the sun.

Maude studied Irma's photograph and realized that Irma resembled her slightly. Yes, there was a distinct resemblance. One of these days, she decided, I'll go to a park or to one of those piers on the West side wearing only my skimpiest bathing suit, and then, among all the freaks and weirdos with their Great Danes, I'll stretch out on a bench, my eyes shut, soaking in the sun, oblivious to everything and everyone around me . . .

When Gregory had stepped out of their apartment to walk across to the Light Gallery he was wearing a blue gingham shirt she had bought him for his thirty-eighth birthday, and the blue blazer she had bought him at Tripler's. She had spotted it in the shopwindow. She had not even intended to buy him anything that day. Yes, he said, when he tried it on. It's a nifty jacket. She had also bought him three silk shirts, two ties, and a belt. Seeing him for the first time, a woman, any woman, might think that Gregory was a really sexy sort of guy. He loved to leave women with that impression.

6

Maude is quite prepared to acknowledge that the instability of every object around her, the instability of her vision, the instability of her fragile demands upon herself and others may have paved the way to what had happened between them, at the same time that it steeled her for the eventuality of Gregory's abrupt departure. Perhaps *un-announced* was the word for which she was searching, not *abrupt*. His departure being unannounced appeared as abrupt. He left saying that he was going to take in a show at the Light Gallery. The mere mention of the gallery brought to mind the acquisition of the photograph, and then the presence of the photographer in their apartment, a somewhat hostile presence, she felt.

She watches Gregory leave, and with the aid of his binoculars follows his progress across the park. Most likely he will proceed straight to the Light Gallery, but the possibility that he will fail to return cannot be ruled out. . . . He'll do anything to demolish her, destroy her, intensify the agony she suffers daily at the instability, the fragility, the ambiguity, the indirectness of everything that is said and done.

But despite the aforementioned instability of her vision, she can easily run up a flight of stairs,
she can also sew on a button,
prepare a mushroom omelette,
calmly undress in front of an open window,
grip a head between her thighs,
turn her head ever so slightly to the left and then to the right at the dinner table
and gravely listen to what the men on either side of her are saying.
What else can she do?
Afflicted with the grave insecurity that measures the exact, the precise breaking point of every object, she can also muffle her screams.
She can wait in a panic for Gregory's return.
She can kill some time by writing a letter to her father who is spending the summer as usual in his run-down country place.

7

This is an introduction to the father. His left eye twitches at what appear to be regular intervals. But his handwriting is quite controlled, quite steady, almost appearing confident and overbearing. Wherever he happens to be, he is waiting for the mailman, waiting for the envelope bearing her nervous scrawl.

Why am I writing this letter to my father, Maude asks herself. I am writing this letter to cause him pain.

It is one of those beautiful days in early June or late August. In one week Maude has received half-a-dozen picture postcards from friends vacationing abroad. Most of the postcards show a good deal of blue sky, an excessive amount when you come to think of it. It is the color so dearly loved by the suntanned men and women stretched out on the white beach, their blank-looking faces turned skywards. The postcards she receives are all cheerfully cryptic. If you only knew who is screwing Lou. P and S have separated again. He is trying to persuade me to leave F. Who is Lou. Who is P and S. And who is F? The postcards allude to exotic Persian rituals in the caves. The cards are all addressed to her and Gregory, it being taken for granted that they, for the time being at least, are still sharing the same perfect apartment overlooking Central Park. That they are still sharing the same magnificent blue-tiled bathroom with the sunken tub, and that occasionally, when the situation demands it, they compare each other favorably to someone else, someone who may have suddenly cropped up in their life, someone who smiled at one of them invitingly, a smile that could not have been mistaken for anything else . . . For all Maude knows, everyone who has been writing and calling her on the phone may know more about the woman in the photograph than she does. For all she knows, Gregory may at this moment be seeing the woman. It might have been he who requested the photographer to take the photograph of the woman in the black bathing suit. Nothing could possibly surprise her now.

All the same, despite her almost detached awareness of Gregory's ongoing unfaithfulness (what an old-fashioned word) she is mistaken in her belief that anything she might write her father could possibly cause him pain. He is inured to her attempts to cause him pain, because he recognizes her intent to do so. No, her letter will not cause him pain. When someone stole his new bike, that caused him pain, and when the tomatoes he planted were waterlogged, that caused him pain, and whenever he missed a train back to the city, it would cause him a terrible and agonizing pain.

What is her father doing at this precise moment. He is working on his eighteenth novel. His principal character, Agnes, a divorcee, is walking along Madison Avenue, musing to herself as she glances at the more attractive shopwindows. It would never, for instance, occur to Maude's father to question the fragility of glass, or ponder the intrinsic function of the large plate-glass windows in a post industrial society.

Not unlike his daughter, his character Agnes can run up a flight of stairs,
sew on a button,
prepare a spinach pie for seven,
toss a vase across the room,
set the dial correctly on the small washing machine in the kitchen,
and determinately search for a specific word in the dictionary, a word that would spell a certain release, that would indicate a lightening of the burden some people suddenly, when they least expect it, feel in their hearts, or roughly in the area where they suspect their hearts to be, somewhere below the left shoulder, and a bit to the right.

Like his daughter, his character, Agnes, can lightheartedly chat for hours on the phone with her best friend. It is part of the novel's format. The conversation may appear banal, but it is pertinent to the novel's development. Still, Maude's father is terribly selective in his choice of details he wishes to magnify and details he wishes to omit. If the doorman is about to collapse, and if Agnes, his character, mistakenly presses the wrong elevator button, he neglects to mention it. He glosses over the universal dread people have that someone may change the locks on their doors while they are out. All his male characters are somewhat heavy-handed but brave. They seem to show a marked preference for fur collars on their wintercoats, and stare expectantly at the naked woman in their bedroom. The woman, in this case, is Agnes. She is standing proudly (?) erect, her legs slightly parted. All the men agree that she has superb legs. Fleshy calves. In chapter three of his eighteenth novel, Agnes is about to be screwed. This she knows. She anticipates it. One might say she was aware of it the moment she woke up that morning. It will happen today, she said to herself. Not that she could possibly anticipate it all in its minute details, but only in a broad sense that did not, however, diminish the clarity of her vision of the event that was to take place. It could happen at any moment. She may, for the duration of the climactic encounter, lie on her back, or sit on a tabletop, or crouch on the floor. The positions, for that is what they are called, are as recognizable as the objects that are so carefully and meticulously displayed in any one of the shopwindows on Madison Avenue. A woman can easily spend an hour selecting a blouse, asking herself: Shall I buy this one or that. A woman can always recognize a beautiful blouse. A woman can also recognize a prick, even in its flaccid state. Each recognition presents a different problem to the mind. What is my correct response, asks the character in her father's novel. Clearly it is to arouse the man. In doing so, the man, as it were, recedes into the background, becoming one with the wallpaper, as Agnes concentrates her entire attention on the man's prick.

If only all my father's female characters did not resemble me, sighed Maude.

As stated previously, the unreliability of Maude's vision, the unreliability of each telephone conversation she has, the unreliability of every encounter with a friend, acquaintance, or past lover, has prepared Maude for Gregory's disappearance. It was really astonishing, when she thought of it, that his disappearance had not occurred at an earlier date. That he had waited five-and-a-half years to disappear. A few characters in her father's novels had on one occasion or another dropped out of sight, but they were all minor characters, and never missed by the reader. Evidently her father had no use for disappearances. He did not care to create ambiguous situations that required a great deal of explanations. Instinctively, he understood the readers' distaste for the gratuitous act. He knew his women readers, and his readers were predominantly women. He interviewed them in the supermarket. A woman was not bewildered when she saw a naked man in front of her. She can readily accept in a man's excitement the great need that manifests itself daily in all human beings. A woman can to a great extent determine her own response to that need.
   She can run up a flight of stairs,
undress,
examine herself in the mirror with narrowed eyes,
and ask herself: Will they like me?
before entering the adjacent room where the two men she had met an hour earlier are waiting.

It is taken for granted that a woman has certain preferences.
   She prefers one bedspread to another,
one man to another,
one position to another,
one picture frame to another,

although at times all things tend to blur, to become indistinct, so that each choice
becomes increasingly difficult.

What would Maude say if asked, what is it that you now want most?

8

Are you aware, Gregory had told Maude shortly after they were married, that all the women in your father's novels are exact replicas of you. They're all highly sexed women with splendid legs who tend to be nearsighted. They all seem to spend a good deal of time writing lengthy confessional letters to their father. She hadn't noticed until Gregory brought it to her attention. If not for Gregory she would still be reading her father's novels without a clue as to the true identity of his principal female characters. In her father's latest novel, Agnes, the ash-blond divorcee was gazing raptly at a shopwindow on Madison Avenue when a young athletic-looking man with a slightly protruding cleft chin stopped at her side, to contemplate the objects that were on view behind the thick plate-glass window. She felt her pulse quicken. The two of them stared at the imported leather suitcases, the leather briefcases, the leather handbags, the gloves, hats, slippers, all of leather, and all imported. She could see his face reflected on the shopwindow. The protruding cleft chin was a minor flaw, easily overlooked. He wore a winter coat with a fur collar. The coat was unbuttoned, and she could see the vested plaid suit he wore. Coolly he studied her reflection in the plate-glass window, debating whether or not to speak to her.

At night, alone in bed, Maude tosses about in her sleep. Whose head is she gripping between her thighs. Is it Gregory's, or is it the head of the man in the winter coat with the fur collar?

Although the world is filled with doubtful and dubious information, a woman can tell at once when a man is trying to pick her up. A woman, by the time she reaches thirty, has seen her share of men, dressed and undressed, singlemindedly striding towards her. It is consistent with this single-minded sexual pursuit that a woman will daily, sometimes hourly, examine herself in the bedroom or bathroom mirror with narrowed eyes, asking herself: Will he like me?

Everytime we fuck, Gregory once confided to Maude, with a slight almost imperceptible grimace of distaste, I feel as if I am one of the characters in your father's latest novel.

Why the detestation, Maude asks herself. Does he dislike me, or does he merely dislike the women in Dad's novels, in which event I could try to persuade Dad to alter them somewhat, to make them less demanding.

9

Please do not be distressed by this letter, she wrote her father. I really expect Gregory to return within the hour. He went to have a look at the latest photographic exhibition at the Light Gallery on Madison. An hour after he left I fixed myself a light lunch. Tomato soup with an egg in it, and a tuna sandwich on rye bread. At four in the morning I called Muriel. I had to speak to someone. I would have preferred to speak to you, but I know how you hate to have anyone call you when you are at work, and I can never tell when you're not either at work on your novel or asleep.

Gregory left Maude on a Tuesday. He walked out of the apartment just as she was getting ready to plan her day. He looked his usual unconcerned self as he stepped out of their eight-room apartment on the eighteenth floor, an apartment containing two color tv sets, approximately eight thousand books and two thousand records. Most of the books had been signed by their authors. To Gregory with the deepest gratitude, and such shit.

When Maude runs into an acquaintance in the park who inquires what she has been doing with herself, Maude replies: I am presently working on a long letter.

10

Writers receive long letters with grave misgivings, particularly when the letter appears to have been written by a close member of the family. Lengthy letters have a way of becoming books. They are a pretext to enable the letter's author to enter the combative world of literature. How many people have squeezed their unwelcome presence into literary history just by writing a long revealing letter to their father.

I fully comprehend, wrote Maude to her father, that when Gregory went off to see the exhibition at the Light Gallery, it may not yet have dawned on him that he might not return. I clearly recall saying: Give me half-an-hour, and I'll get dressed and come with you. No, no, he said. He was only going to take a quick look at some photographs. On his way back he would pick up the *Times*. I never saw the *Times* that day. I was so certain he would get it. The next day I couldn't get a copy of Tuesday's *Times*, for love or money. When I called Muriel, she at once asked me what's wrong. I asked her if she had Tuesday's *Times*. She said no.

I think you are well rid of Gregory, Muriel had said. What you need is a stable, strong, and emotional man.
No, said Maude. What I now need is a smaller apartment.

What I now need is a smaller apartment, she writes her father. I also need a place to store the books and records. Could you possibly take a few days off and drive over in the station wagon. You always wanted that entire set of Maupassant. Remember!

How odd, thinks Maude, that under the circumstances I am not discontent. How odd that I did not become a prisoner of my marriage to Gregory. How bizarre that he should have walked out of my life on a Tuesday before breakfast. How fortunate I am not to have any children to worry about. The oddest thing of all was the fact that she could no longer remember his face. It worried her. Poor Gregory's face had been effaced from her memory. Try as she did she could not put Gregory's handsome face together in her mind. She managed the lips and the eyebrows and even the hair, but she could not assemble the total face. The total face escaped her. She succeeded, however, at the first try with the face of the young photographer, thinking to herself, what a sweet face. I bet he's an awfully sweet guy.

11

This is an introduction to the nervous handwriting of Maude. She is sitting at her little writing desk, writing a long letter to her father. She

35

can see her father in his large rather neglected country house impatiently waiting for the mailman, impatiently waiting for her letter. Her father is wearing his old Harris tweed. He and the mailman go through their familiar routine, speaking about the weather, the crops, the livestock, before the mailman reluctantly hands over the mail.

She could have typed her letter, but she preferred to write it by hand, infecting the desperate message her letter conveyed with the angular nervousness of her handwriting. Her handwriting accentuated the intensity of her feelings. It clamored for attention. It also demanded an immediate sympathetic response.

Everything that you see and hear is plausible, her father had once said. At the same time, it can also remain highly questionable. All the things in this house, the house included, more or less reflect a certain taste. Is it my taste? Take this couch, for instance. Why is it still here when it should have been sitting in the garbage dump years ago? If I were to sit down and write about the couch I would probably write that I was attached to it, in order to make plausible its presence in my study.

In her letter Maude casually mentions that Gregory had briefly stepped out to see an exhibition at the Light Gallery two weeks ago. She had intended to accompany him, but he had reminded her that she owed her father a letter. If not for the letter she might have accompanied Gregory to the gallery. In the late afternoon, when Gregory failed to return, she called the gallery, identifying herself as the lady who some time ago had purchased a print of the Great Mosque of Kairouan. She wondered if there were any other prints left of the Mosque, and incidentally, had her husband, Gregory Brinn, been in that day to purchase another photograph of the lady in the one-piece bathing suit sunning herself on a park bench?

12

Every evening Maude walks naked to a window and takes a deep breath. She is relaxing. She is also asking herself: What will I do tonight? She can always take in a movie, or go to a concert, or see a play, or read a good book, or watch an old movie on TV, or do some

Yoga exercises, or bake a cake. She can also, on the spur of the moment, invite someone to dinner.

Are you free tonight, she asked me on the phone. I thought you might like to come over for dinner. I know this is terribly impromptu. You can bring your friend. The woman in the photograph. Oh, by the way, Gregory is away on business. It'll just be the two or three of us.

She can also go to one of the neighborhood bars and strike up a conversation with a stranger, someone who will undoubtedly have read one if not more of her father's eighteen books. Whenever she mentions her maiden name, the response is immediate: Good God, you're the daughter of Emmanuel F. Hugo. I firmly believe he's the greatest writer since Maupassant. She used to have her father read Maupassant to her when she was a child. The mere mention of Maupassant makes her weep. She is weeping for her childhood.

She can also, just to show that she doesn't give the slightest damn, throw a gigantic party, inviting all her friends and their friends, and just people her friends may know or run into.
I've been looking for you, she said severely. I was afraid that you mightn't show up. I don't know half of these people. Did you bring her along? I introduced Irma to Maude.
Why did I bring Irma along?
Did I want her to see her photograph in Gregory's study?
Did I want her to see the view from the eighteenth floor?
Did I want her to savor the perfection of the apartment? The perfection of every object in the apartment? The perfection, consequently, attained by her photograph in being in such close proximity to the other carefully selected objects in the study.

Goodnight. Maude kissed me on the lips. I left without Irma. I couldn't locate her in the dense crowd. Thank you for bringing her, said Maude.

13

On the spur of the moment I decided to throw a large party, Maude writes her father. It may cause him pain. It is intended to cause him pain. She describes the people who came to her party, she also describes Irma, describes her in a way to cause her father anguish.

Maude likes to write letters. She's quite an accomplished letter writer. The letters are breezy, informative, and even witty. She likes to make fun of herself. Once, when she and Gregory had spent a week in Jamaica she wrote her father how while they had been making love the door of their hotel room was opened by the chambermaid. Just put it on the table, Gregory had said without even turning around. The maid placed his polished shoes on the table and quickly stepped out of their room. They burst out laughing hysterically as soon as the maid had left, but when her father made use of the incident in one of his novels, Gregory actually threatened to take him to court. He's really totally humorless, said her father. My poor child, married to a humorless man.

She had married a man who was a major literary critic, as well as an authority on Maupassant, because it was so refreshing to be close to someone who could analyze so thoughtfully all the women characters in her father's books. Of course, that one is you too, Gregory would say. Can't you see how your father is trying to disguise her to lead us astray. That first year she spent with Gregory was the most exciting time in her life. Suddenly she was able to cope with her fear that the elevator might go out of control and plunge eighteen floors to the basement.

I wonder what I should do with all the books the publishers keep sending to Gregory, she asked me. I didn't feel like inquiring if she had seen Irma since the party. It wasn't any of my business. I realized that for the second time I had received an invitation from one of the Brinns that was given in bad faith. Maude had wanted me to bring Irma to her, and I had complied.

Why? Why? Why?

14

Without the slightest trepidation Maude enters the room in which the two men are sitting on the couch with Irma. No one prevents her from walking to the window and looking at the West Side Drive, as she pretends not to notice that the two are quite openly caressing Irma's small white breasts, breasts that resemble her own breasts. In order not to see the men and Irma, Maude is compelled to partly close her eyes, or focus them elsewhere, on the wallpaper for instance. It is a pity about the wallpaper. The wallpaper destroys the room. It makes the room smaller and less attractive. Obviously Irma had little sense for color or design. Maude would have suggested a bolder pattern. But Irma had an incredible body. Most men noticed her body. Irma, àt their first encounter, had quite casually mentioned that her legs were her best feature. What an amazing thing to say, Maude had thought at the time. For some reason the two men were not touching Irma's legs. Perhaps, it occurred to Maude, they were saving Irma's legs for later. Perhaps they were satisfied to look at the legs while concentrating on other parts of Irma's anatomy. Who can say? Who can tell what is on the mind of a man who is caressing a woman. One of the two men was rather attractive. He had bony hands and blue eyes. For no discernable reason he looked at Maude and said: I expect to make a lot of money next year. At least twenty thousand. Maude was not impressed. Her father made eight times as much after taxes each year. She watched the two men, who might easily have stepped out of one of her father's novels, strip Irma naked. She had expected Irma to offer a certain amount of resistance. A certain struggle was called for, Maude felt. Instead, all she saw was total compliance. It is depressing, she thought, to see an attractive woman give in so easily. In her father's books the women always put up a certain struggle. Even in Maupassant it was not merely, one, two, three. Is Irma, she wondered, without backbone. She tries to stifle a yawn. Her yawn is an unabashed admission that she is becoming bored by the spectacle and by her role as captive audience. She is thirty-five and easily bored, but she makes no move to leave the apartment. She knows what would happen if she did. She knows how the men would respond.

I can take a taxi home, thinks Maude. She is disconcerted to find Irma staring at her. It's not more than ten, at the most fourteen steps to the door, another twelve to the elevator.

She would describe what had taken place in a letter to her father. She would go into great detail to cause him anguish. I was afraid, she would write, I was so afraid, and yet, I was also excited, so excited.

Her father wrote big fat American books. At this moment he is sitting at his typewriter turning out beautiful books for America. He is a man of letters. He is a man America respects. He is a man who understands the quintessential American need for friendship. It is this fundamental understanding that has enabled him to sell his books in the hundred thousands. People crave friendship, not sex. Her father's face is recognized by millions. Each time he takes the BMT he is besieged by the readers of his books. She adores her father. She adores the poignant titles of his books. Books, in which all the principal female characters resemble her. It is only to be expected, she thinks. She can also recognize the figure of her father in his books: Her father at the age of four, seven, eighteen, twenty-two, forty-nine, sixty-seven, eighty-one, one-hundred-and-two.

15

Maude is compelled to concede that one of the two men, the more agreeable-looking one, is screwing Irma in her presence. She stares at Irma's face in amazement. It is a face she can no longer recognize. It could be me, thinks Maude, how easily it could be me.

Where the hell have you been, shouted Gregory furiously when she got back to her apartment at four A.M. I've been going stark raving mad. He kept pounding the table as he spoke. She had never seen him looking so agitated. I want an explanation.

You . . . you . . . you dare ask me where I have been. Her voice was quivering with indignation. You've been gone for over two weeks.

Oh, no, cried Gregory. Not again. It's going to be one of those long drawn out melodramas. I can't take it. I simply can't take it. Not at four in the morning.

16

I really don't know why you want me to take your photograph in a black bathing suit in a park, but if you insist, I will.

It's a going away present, Maude explained.

A parting shot, I said.

I like the view from the eighteenth floor. I like everything about this apartment. From Gregory's desk I can see Central Park, and when I turn my head slightly to the left sitting on the second shelf is a photograph I took some time ago. My father-in-law wants to use it on the cover of his next book. Sure, I said, if Maude doesn't object.

Maude, naked as usual, enters my room.

ARDOR/AWE/ATROCITY

Her car, an old Dodge station wagon, developed engine trouble as she was driving along Route 15, traversing the bleakest and most desolate part of the Mojave Desert. She slowed down to twenty miles an hour and listened to the knocking, the persistent knocking sound that came from the engine. A sign[57] she had passed a few miles back indicated that it was forty miles to the next gasoline station. Rather than stop and wait for someone to assist her, she decided to continue at a reduced speed. Now and then a car, traveling at a great speed, shot[56] past her. It did not appear as if the road was patrolled by the police. As soon as she spotted the man standing at the side of the road, waving a sign[57] at her, she stepped on the gas, afraid that otherwise, in this absolute wilderness, he might try to wrench open[43] the car door. The crudely hand-made sign[57] he was holding read: GOING MY WAY? EL LAY. She was too preoccupied with her own problems, her own apprehensions, to wonder how[22] the man came to be where he was, although the words he yelled[74] at her, you[73] silly cunt, kept reverberating in her ears long after she had lost sight of him in the rearview[64] mirror. There was no sign[57] of life on the rugged terrain to her left or right. Lost in her thoughts, she did not see the immense billboard looming ahead until she was almost on top of it. A freshly cut[9] half of an orange, displayed in the center of the billboard, floated against a bright dayglow yellow background. Beneath the orange the word PLEASURE[46] stood out in large red letters. By now she had turned off the air conditioning for fear that it might place an additional burden on the malfunctioning engine. Out of nowhere a fairly large-sized gray furry animal darted across her car's path. She came to a screeching halt in time to see the animal limp off to her left, leaving a thin trail of blood on the highway.

BUOYANT[4] / BOB[5] / BODY[6]

The large buoyant-looking[4] man in the red-checked shirt who had approached her in the motel dining room was taken away by the police, and so was the young man who received a deep[11] cut[9] in his arm as a result of the altercation that had taken place between the two of them. He'll be all right, the motel owner assured her, after the young man, blood dripping[10] from his left arm, was driven to a nearby hospital. It was on my account, she thought. The young man had actually risked his life for her. She intended to get his name and address, but the rudeness of the motel owner's wife, who seemed to be blaming her for the incident of the night before, and her own desire to leave the motel as quickly as possible, may have been the reason why she completely forgot about it until she was some thirty miles away. To her great relief, the knocking sound of the engine had somewhat subsided. She blamed herself for smiling back at the man in the red-checked shirt, and not realizing that he might misinterpret her friendly smile as a sign[57] of interest on her part.

CALIFORNIA[7] / COLOR[8] / CUT[9]

Jane[28] called her parents on an impulse from a rest stop later that day. When her mother answered the phone, Jane,[28] as if to prevent her mother from raising any of the issues that would cause the two of them to quarrel,[51] immediately launched herself into a detailed description of the landscape around her, the magnificent colors[8] of the sunset she was witnessing that very second, and the marvelous people she had met on the way. She also mentioned that she intended to send her mother dupes of the slides she had taken all along the way. I feel no regret whatever at leaving, she kept repeating.

If I only knew what was going on in your[73] mind, her mother said.

Mom, said Jane[28] quietly. Once you[73] see the slides you'll[73] know exactly what's on my mind. Before hanging up, Jane[28] said that she and Dorothy were taking turns at the wheel.

Can I just say a word to Dorothy, said her mother. Why can't I ever speak to Dorothy?

DRIP[10] / DEEP[11] / DELIGHT[12]

She is lying naked on the bed. Her heart is beating wildly. This is absolutely ridiculous, she thinks. There is no reason to feel nervous, uncertain, or afraid. Her battered-looking car is parked outside between two perpendicular white[68] lines. Her face is thrust into the soft pillow . . . as she clings to the smell of the freshly laundered white[68] pillowcase. The wall-to-wall rug in the room is an off-white,[68] the tiles in the bathroom are white,[68] so is the washbasin, the bathroom ceiling, and the Venetian blinds. Knees[31] are for supporting the body[6] in a crouching position[48] as the man who is holding her by the waist thrusts[58] himself into her again and again. Both she and the man are committed to complete silence. Each is immersed in his own watchfulness as the bodies[6] acquire greater and greater independence, disregarding the instructions they keep receiving from their separate centers of communication, their minds.

ERECTION[13] / EXOTIC[14] / EARTHQUAKE[15]

Jane[28] is watching a rerun of "Mannix" on the color[8] TV in her room. It is a cheap set and everything is depicted in the most garish colors[8] on the screen. Intently she watches a pink-faced Mannix, gun[21] drawn, racing along the length of a red-tiled rooftop of a stylish hacienda. Now[40] and then the camera settles briefly on the familiar Southern California[7] background of palm trees, swimming pool, exotic[14] plants, an interior filled with massive pieces of modern furniture, glass-topped[20] tables, large plate-glass[20] windows that permit the blue sky to function as a fourth wall in the room. For the past three days she has noticed an oily substance dripping[10] from the left front axle of her car. The mechanic at the garage assured her it was nothing. Each time she pulls out, she leaves a shiny black stain on the ground. What possibly can she be afraid of?

FUTURE[16] / FLINCH[17] / FUCK[18]

I'd love to stay and watch "Mannix" with you,[73] said the man as he left. Perhaps another time? She locked[35] the door and returned to the TV. Her keys[32] lay on the dresser. There were at least a dozen keys[32] on the key[32] chain, but only the keys[32] to the car and the keys[32] of her two valises were of any use to her now.[40] For some reason she can't get herself to discard the now[40] usless bunch of keys.[32] She looks at them carefully, trying to recall which key[32] opened which door. How[22] many times has Mannix, like any other Southern Californian,[7] casually pulled out his keys[32] and opened[43] the door to his office, only to be assaulted, or compelled at gun[21] point to leave the office and enter another man's car? Of course, Mannix is aging gradually. He is losing some of his erstwhile youthfulness[75] and his former bounce, but is he also growing careless? Jane[28] counted her traveler's checks while watching "Mannix." Is Mannix at all capable of having a good time? Or has he come to represent the stern inner-driven justice-oriented force of retribution that Southern Californians[7] need to stabilize their nervous systems, thereby enabling their brain cells to exercise a minimum amount of control as they drive their cars on the six-lane highways into and out of L.A.

GLEAMING[19] / GLASS[20] / GUN[21]

The newspapers and magazines, available in English and Spanish, report with varying degrees of accuracy the whereabouts and activities of people whose names are instantly recognized by every Southern Californian.[7] In that respect the newspapers and magazines are a kind of pleasure[46] map[37] for the people. They also provide the answer to the frequently raised question:[50] How[22] is it all done? People watch Mannix carefully, in order better to emulate the wealthy people he frequently visits in the graceful-looking haciendas of San Diego. Without Mannix, Southern California[7] would have no entrée to the wealth and power in L.A. and San Diego. Without Mannix Southern California[7] would be bereft of the distinction between ardor,[1] awe,[2] and atrocity.[3] When Mannix grimaces with distaste as he visits the city morgue to view[64] a badly beaten body of a woman,[67] he spells out, for everyone's gratification, the interdependent relationship of *Justice* and *Good Taste*.

The question bears repeating. How[22] is it all done? How[22] is this miraculous way of life accomplished? The highway system is just one of the answers. The vast intricate[26] network[42] of roads in Southern California[7] facilitate the filming or, as it is sometimes called, the shooting[56] of a "Mannix" sequel of sixty minutes minus time for commercials. It is done, incidentally, despite the omnipresent fear of earthquakes,[15] despite the heat,[24] despite the smog, despite the collisions on the road. Mannix's hands firmly grip the steering wheel as the other car attempts to overtake Mannix's immaculate[25] white[68] convertible with the telephone that links him to his girl Friday and the nervous system of all of Southern California.[7] The car pulls abreast and side-swipes Mannix's car. A bullet smashes his windshield,[69] narrowly missing his head. There is not a pair of adult hands in Southern California[7] that have not experienced the electric flow of fear from the brain to the fingers gripping the wheel, as a collision at eighty miles an hour with another car is barely avoided.

Jane[28] sitting in the soft comfortable beige leather[34] seat next to the driver glances at the two large diamond rings on the manicured plumpish fingers of the woman[67] behind the wheel. The woman[67] is wearing a striped silk blouse, a white[68] linen skirt, and white[68] shoes.

My dear, she says in a somewhat patronizing voice to Jane,[28] I simply insist that you[73] stay with us. Maxwell[39] would be furious if you[73] didn't. We have so much room in the house. By Eastern standards the house is small, perhaps deceptively small. It overlooks[44] the ocean. In the driveway are two gleaming[19] cars. Everything is a bit showy. A bit too finished. When Jane[28] calls her home in the evening, her parents sing Happy Birthday to her. Briefly, but only briefly, she loses control, as the tears well up in her eyes.

IMMACULATE[25]/INTRICATE[26]/IMAGE[27]

What is she thinking as she opens[43] a checking account at the bank in the new shopping center. She hasn't looked at a newspaper in weeks. The occasional light tremor under her feet is accepted the way a bullet that narrowly missed Mannix and hit his friend instead is accepted, with resignation, with foreknowledge. In a boutique located in the large shopping complex, they accept her check after glancing at her out-of-state driver's license. She buys herself some underwear,[62] a blouse, clogs, sunglasses,[20] a bikini, all for less than two hundred dollars. Every time anyone hears a siren in Southern California[7] he or she immediately thinks of Mannix, seeing him sprint up a hill, a perfect target for the gunmen[21] on top.

JANE[28]/ JET[29]/ JEWEL[30]

The American male arriving in L.A. goes to the nearest drugstore for some aspirin and a Coke. He goes to a liquor store for a bottle of Scotch. He stops at the first motel along his way and grabs a few hours of sleep. This is Southern California.[7] The women[67] here have experienced everything at least once in their minds. They do not flinch[17] when the word fuck[18] is used. Jane[28] doesn't flinch[17] or recoil when Helen tells her, you[73] mustn't reject Maxwell,[39] he'll be so hurt.

KNEES[31]/ KEYS[32]/ KILLED[33]

A row of palm trees in front of a three-story apartment building. Not a soul in sight. Mannix parks his car on the circular gravel driveway and unhurriedly walks to the entrance of the building. Everyone in Southern California[7] knows why Mannix is about to enter the apartment building, but no one knows what to expect. Anything can happen next. The realism[53] of the moment engraves itself upon the brain. Everything Mannix undertakes[63] to do is highly plausible. Everyone watching Mannix is captivated, as each action, each succeeding event, feeds the brain's expectations, expectations that are based on strict standards, strict Southern California[7] standards of conduct and behavior. Jane[28] is sitting on a leather[34] couch. Do her legs meet with Maxwell's[39] approval. Are they sufficiently erotic. Is Maxwell,[39] in his mind, trying to control the movement of her legs. Maxwell[39] continues to stare at her. His look can be said to be filled with expectation. Does Jane[28] accept the inherent femininity of her situation. Has she become a part of Maxwell's[39] scenario for the afternoon. Does the bright Southern California[7] landscape intensify her response to his elaborately planned endeavor, his somewhat mechanical ardor.[1] No bullet shot[56] intervenes as she, embracing him with her legs, responds to the realism[53] of his smooth performance.

LEATHER[34] / LOCK[35] / LANDING[36]

I would never marry a cop, Jane[28] tells Maxwell[39] as they are lying on her bed. And I would never marry a California[7] cop.

How about a lawyer?

I'm sick of lawyers as well. Her new blouse is slightly creased. How long have you[73] and Helen been married, she asks.

About twelve years. I was still in the air force when we met.

I didn't know you[73] were in the air force. Were you[73] a pilot?

Did you[73] ever make it with two guys? he asked her suddenly.

The speed at which Californians travel on the six-lane highways ties them to the perpetual *now*,[40] the perpetual *present* in their brains. Jane[28] shuts her eyes. She is alone in this comfortable room, in this elegant house, alone with a spectacular view[64] of the Pacific Ocean and the California[7] sky, alone except for the slightly balding middle-aged head of a man between her legs who is draining her brain of images.[27]

MAPS[37] / MESSAGE[38] / MAXWELL[39]

Jane[28] spoke to the young man she had met on the beach about her trip from New York to L.A. She became quite excited when she described her stay in the motel where the knifing had occurred. She also described her old and now[40] abandoned car in some detail, as if the car, this vehicle[65] that had transported her and her possessions to the West Coast, had not merely been a car, but a treasured[59] possession. . . No, a treasured[59] friend that had aged and then died.

I could have nursed it along for another five thousand miles, she heard herself saying. The young man wore a gold bracelet on his left wrist. It was not politeness or shyness or diffidence that gave his face that particularly attractive look. He seemed to be waiting for her to continue her description, but for all she knew he might be waiting for her to make some kind of a proposal. It was hard[23] to tell.

How do you[73] like it here? she asked.

Here? He seemed taken aback by the question.

She stretched out on the sand. Everything was so exquisite. The people were so beautiful. The sand was soft and white.[68] Very[66] lightly he ran his forefinger up and down the inside of her arm. Later, in her room, he remarked almost casually: I've never had an erection,[13] but there are so many ways to play. Her new TV set was turned off. She could not turn to "Mannix" for guidance. The information on the sixteen-inch screen was *zero*.[78]

NOW[40] / NORMAL[41] / NETWORK[42]

With each new shopping center, with each new airport, with each new office building complex, Southern California[7] is expanding the range of the plausible. The immediate future,[16] the immediate immaculate[25] future[16] lies mapped[37] out in the brain cells as the suntanned people on the Coast carefully observe Mannix's arrival at an airport. It resembles their own arrival at an airport; it also resembles, to tell the truth, the arrival of Bob[5] Down. The uneventful landing[36] of the jet,[29] the debarkation, the metal-and-glass[20] terminal, the white[68] formica counters, and the blue-uniformed stewardesses in the airport cafeteria are all, more or less, devoid of surprise.[55] Keeping an eye on Mannix is one way of watching the smoothly functioning process of a culture prepared for any eventuality, any disaster—waves of heart attacks, incendiary devices about to explode, poison gas, earthquakes,[15] a lion escaping from the zoo,[76] engine breakdown, plane out of control, members of the radical underground wishing to be reunited with their parents. For Bob[5] Down it is the familiar world. Only it is warmer and brighter. Waiting to pick up his luggage he spots Jane[28] just as she is leaving the main terminal together with a tall blond man. Barely controlling his excitement, he runs after her, yelling:[74] Jane,[28] Jane,[28] stop, stop . . . and then, having caught up with her, embraces her enthusiastically, saying: What a beautiful surprise.[55] No one told me that you[73] were in California.[7]

OPEN[43] / OVERLOOKS[44] / OBLIGATION[45]

Still feeling surprised[55] and baffled by Jane's uncharacteristically cool response to his spontaneous and warm greeting, Bob[5] Down returns to the luggage carousel upon which his two brand new suitcases, by now the only luggage left on the carousel, are completing another full circle. Controlling a temptation to stop at the airport bar for a drink, Bob[5] Down, luggage in hand, heads for the nearest exit. When he had asked Jane[28] for her telephone number, she had responded as if he were prying into her life. Bob[5] had taken an instant dislike to the man she was with. Jane[28] had not asked him a single question; she had also neglected to introduce him to the man at her side. She had not been flustered or startled when he, Bob,[5] had rushed forward to greet her. She might have been vaguely annoyed. I'm sort of in a rush, she said finally, as if to explain her rudeness. The man accompanying her had not said a word. Bob[5] kept seeing the tall slender man at Jane's[28] side, kept seeing the black silk or nylon long-sleeved shirt he wore, the shirt unbuttoned[61] to reveal a large expanse of a tanned hairless chest, and a delicate gold chain at the end of which was attached a small ivory figure with a disproportionately large phallus. He told himself that is was ridiculous to attach any significance[57] to this encounter.

The next day when Bob[5] called the number Jane[28] had so reluctantly given him, a disembodied female voice repeated the last four digits of the number he had dialed. It turned out to be an answering service. He left his hotel number and a message[38] for Jane,[28] requesting her to call him at her convenience. The tiny totemic[60] figurine dangling from the end of the chain around the man's neck came to mind each time he thought of Jane.[28] What about it was so distasteful?

PLEASURE[46]/ PUNISH[47]/ POSITION[48]

At what stage does the Southern Californian[7] convert the world around him into the flatness that resembles a movie screen. Everything the mind focuses on may be something it might have, on a prior occasion, spotted on a screen. In time, the Southern Californian[7] will no longer ask, can I also do it? Instead he or she will want to know where, at what movie house, can it be seen?

Bob[5] Down quit[49] his job, sold his car, his antique leather[34] couch, and his collection of weather vanes, and moved in with a friend in New York City, prior to leaving for the West Coast. He had been planning to make this move for a long time. California,[7] why California,[7] his friends wanted to know. Why California,[7] asked his parents. They refused to acknowledge that they knew next to nothing about their son. They hardly know anything about each other. They are a secretive family in the true American tradition. Everything is on display, everything in their life and in their house in Princeton, New Jersey, is visible, to be seen, noticed, acknowledged. Everything: diplomas, photographs, scuffed Oriental carpets, letters from the college president, slippers, stuffed animals, toilet articles, trophies, the bottles in the liquor cabinet, several rifle awards, mementos from Egypt, Italy, and Chile. What are they hiding? They are hiding Bob[5] Down, their mysterious son who calls them twice weekly. The first time he mentioned running into Jane.[28] They remembered Jane[28] with a certain disapproval, a certain vague trepidation. Could he have fallen for Jane?[28] I wonder if he's sleeping with her, said Bob's[5] mother. Bob's[5] father responded with a manly, ha ha ha. What's wrong with . . . but he doesn't mention the word. He somehow restrains himself from uttering the word. It is a perfect word printed on a page. . . . But he doesn't want to be responsible for what might happen to his wife if he used the word in her presence.

QUIT[49] / QUESTION[50] / QUARREL[51]

Mr. and Mrs. Down watch "Mannix" on Saturday at nine. They are glued to their seats as they watch "Mannix," hoping to become acquainted with the section of the country where their son is staying. They realize that they needed someone like Mannix to get to the heart of the problem, to determine what was the matter with their son. He must have friends, said Bob's[5] father. Everyone has a friend or two. How[22] many do you have, his wife asked him. They keep watching Mannix and waiting for the phone to ring. When Bob[5] rings, he is his usual cheerful self. He is filled with information. Nothing is hidden. That is what is so disconcerting. Nothing is hidden, but everything is murky. Is he seeing Jane[28] again. Has she left her husband and two children. Should they call her parents and inquire.

RECOGNITION[52] / REAL[53] / REMEMBER[54]

What is the present situation. It is defined by a lack of trust as Mr. and Mrs. Arthur Down pore over the map[37] of L.A. It is a landscape filled with the recollection of Mannix. Buildings, cars, and people age comfortably in the sun. Jane's[28] car is a case in point. She has abandoned it. By now she's come to rely on other people for transportation. By now she knows so many people in Southern California.[7] The bankteller greets her warmly. The guard smiles at her as she leaves. Is there any other way to live? it says on the large billboard advertising sailboats.

SURPRISE[55]/SHOT[56]/SIGN[57]

It is two in the morning, and the four young Chicanos are gaily pushing an abandoned Dodge station wagon down a deserted dead-end street toward the low wood fence behind which there is a sheer drop of forty feet to the water below. One of the four is casually resting his right hand on the steering wheel of the car. As the road begins to dip slightly, the car picks up speed. A minute later all four cheer, Ole, as the car smashes through the fence and plunges downward. In the small bungalows nearby, lights are being turned on. People have no way of knowing if the car contained a body. It is entirely feasible. Everyone of the witnesses has watched "Mannix" at some time or other. The four kids are crowded around the smashed fence, staring down at the wrecked car when the cops arrive. In many respects it is a familiar scene. Guns[21] drawn, the cops push the kids against a nearby wall and frisk them, then handcuffed, they are driven to the police station where they are booked and their possessions religiously entered in a ledger. Four creased wallets, presumably stolen, twenty-one credit cards, all stolen, four knives, handkerchiefs, condoms, a pocket radio, four combs, nail clippers, keys,[32] and approximately two dozen pornographic photographs. On at least six of the photographs Jane's[28] face, Jane's[28] attractive and serious face, is staring unblinkingly at the photographer while she is being screwed. The four kids behind bars have not read Octavio Paz's *The Labyrinth of Solitude,* but they have watched "Mannix." They are fully aware that Mannix has on several occasions managed to break out of jail. But they don't have what Mannix has going for him. They don't have friends in the police department, and they don't have Mannix's white[68] convertible, with the telephone that links him to his secretary, parked conveniently near the station. They know they don't stand a chance. They know the cops aren't xenophiles,[72] they are xenophobes. So they sit in their cell, awake and dreaming of Jane.[28]

THRUST[58]/TREASURED[59]/TOTEMIC[60]

How real[53] is Southern California,[7] people ask themselves daily. The two men who gunned down a guard as they were making their getaway from the bank after the stick-up were also preoccupied with the real.[53] Temporarily the stolen money eased the gnawing sense of uncertainty. By the time Jane[28] arrived to deposit some money in the afternoon, the blood had been wiped up. Everything was back to normal.[41] The suntanned young bankteller seemed more subdued than usual, but the guard who had replaced the guard killed a few hours before smiled broadly at Jane[28] as she was leaving, and said: Have a nice day, Miss. The pictures showing Jane[28] being screwed are still being passed around the police station. Dozens of hard-faced[23] cops grimly memorize her face, her breasts, her legs, her unbelievably erotic positions.[48] Are these real?[53] they ask themselves.

UNBUTTONED[61]/UNDERWEAR[62]/UNDERTAKES[63]

When Bob[5] Down moved into Clark Seedwell's place, he called Jane's[28] answering service to leave his new number. Please, have her call me at her convenience, he said. By now his calling the answering service every time he moved had become a reflex action. When he spoke to his parents, he told them that he was staying with an old friend from college in a rather luxurious house filled with a lot of art and modern furniture. He was making a great many new friends. Since Clark knew an awful lot of people, they led an active social life. To his delight[12] as Clark's new friend he was accepted at once. One Saturday he and Clark went to an exhibition of photographs by a photographer who had once been a close friend of Clark's. Clark didn't really wish to go, but he had a strong sense of duty, of obligation,[45] of doing the correct thing, and he didn't wish to leave the photographer under the impression that he was no longer important to Clark. The photographs were portraits of people Bob[5] Down didn't know. A surprisingly large number of the people photographed wore black leather[34] jackets, and some wore black leather[34] pants as well. Next to each photograph was the name or the names of the persons photographed, and Bob[5] could tell that, although he didn't recognize a single name, the names were well known to most of the people who arrived for the opening, quite a number of them wearing black leather[34] jackets, and looking as if they had just stepped out of one of the photographs on the wall. Clark was at his side when Bob[5] stopped in front of a photograph taken of Clark in a white[68] linen suit, elegant and nonchalant, standing in the corner of a room, while near him on a couch sat a young woman wearing an open black leather[34] jacket, black leather[34] boots, and nothing else. The woman was Jane.[28]

I didn't know that you[73] knew Jane,[28] said Bob.[5]

Surprise,[55] surprise,[55] said Clark.

Her former husband was a schoolmate of mine, explained Bob.[5] I was best man at their wedding.

Did you[73] ever make out with him, asked Clark, laughing at the startled expression on Bob's[5] face.

VIEW[64] / VEHICLE[65] / VERY[66]

The next week Bob[5] and Clark visited Clark's mother in La Jolla, San Diego. In the afternoon, while Clark sat pensively watching from a deck chair, Bob,[5] dressed in whites,[68] played tennis with Clark's mother. She was a slim attractive woman in her early fifties who played an aggressive game. For some reason Bob[5] could not understand, he found that he wished to punish[47] her, taking a great delight in making her race back and forth across the court . . . but punish[47] her for what. For being wealthy, or for being Clark's mother, or for being able to afford this magnificent building and the servants. Or did he resent her taking it for granted the night before that he and Clark would share one bedroom. That evening, Clark's mother said to her son: Did I tell you, Jane[28] was here. She stayed for ever so long . . . She said that she was thinking of returning to New York. She left one morning without even saying good-by. I was relieved to see her go, but it seemed odd that she would leave without a word. What's more, she left her valise behind . . . I hope she's not coming back.

Bob's[5] an old friend of hers, said Clark.

You[73] have such strange friends, said Clark's mother, staring at Bob,[5] and then, as if the idea had just occurred to her: If you're[73] her friend, you[73] must take her valise with you.[73] You're[73] much more likely to run into her than I am.

WOMAN[67]/WHITE[68]/WINDSHIELD[69]

The trouble with people like you,[73] said Clark without bitterness, is that you[73] haven't the vaguest idea of who you[73] would like to fuck,[18] or who you[73] would like to be fucked[18] by, or if at all you[73] would like to fuck,[18] or if possibly you[73] might be able to find some alternative to fucking.[18] Bob[5] piled his luggage into his car. He also carried Jane's[28] suitcase to his car, expecting Clark to protest, but Clark didn't say a word.

I know I owe you[73] a good deal of money, and I intend to repay it as soon as I can.

You're[73] such a bloody asshole, said Clark amiably. I realize that you[73] like to leave a good impression wherever you[73] go. Well, you've[73] done that. I think you're[73] honest, upright, and terribly good-looking. So do all my friends. And who knows, perhaps our mutual friend, Jane,[28] does too. One of these days she'll give you[73] a buzz. Then you[73] can sit down and talk about old times. All those delightful[12] days and nights in Staten Island, or wherever you[73] met.

A short distance from Clark's house Bob[5] picked up a hitchhiker. Lovely day, said Bob[5] pleasantly. One of these lovely days, said the young kid he had picked up, we're going to be hit by the most god-awful quake you[73] ever heard of. At that very precise moment a light tremor shook the ground over which they were passing. Oh fuck[18] it, said Bob,[5] and for the remainder of the ride they did not exchange another word.

X-ED[70]/XEROX[71]/XENOPHILE[72]

Jane's[28] light blue suitcase contained two evening dresses, black lace underwear,[62] a jewel[30] box containing a diamond ring, fourteen thousand dollars in one-hundred-dollar bills, a man's wristwatch, two bank books in her name, a check book in her name, a key[32] to a safe deposit box, about a dozen keys[32] on one large key[32] chain, two dozen Percodan in a small plastic container, a one ounce bag of coke, a Xerox[71] copy of her birth and marriage certificates, a computerized reading of her sign[57] of the zodiac,[77] Virgo the Virgin, the sentence, *a secret meeting will determine your future,*[16] was underlined. Jane[28] had also saved the road maps[37] she used on her trip from New York to L.A. The dozen or so areas x-ed[70] on the map[37] with a red pencil may have been the places where she had stopped overnight. In one of the compartments of the suitcase Bob[5] found a pile of old letters written by a former boyfriend, and several written by her obviously distraught husband, Tom, after she had left him. Bob[5] read the letters hoping to come across some mention of his name, but there was none. In the same compartment next to the letters was an envelope containing several photographs, one of Tom on the Staten Island Ferry standing next to Bob,[5] another of Jane[28] wearing a black bathing suit, sunning herself in a park. In emptying the suitcase, Bob[5] almost overlooked the tiny yellow address book for the most part filled with names of people in the L.A. and San Diego area. He looked up his name and found that each new number he had left with the answering service had been entered in the book. Her parents' telephone number and address were on the first page in the book. On an impulse Bob[5] called their number. Jane's[28] mother answered the phone. She remembered him quite well. He said that he was calling from Princeton. He explained that he hadn't seen Jane[28] in ages and wondered if he could possibly get her number. I haven't heard from her in some time, said Jane's[28] mother. She's making films in Hollywood and has forgotten about us. I can give you[73] a number where you[73] might reach her. If you[73] do, would you[73] please tell her that her Dad died two weeks ago. I'm moving in with my sister in Queens. Jane[28] has her number. Good-by now. I have to get off the line. I have a visitor. Did you[73] say your[73] name was Bob?[5]

YOU[73] / YELLED[74] / YOUTHFULNESS[75]

When Bob[5] called Jane's[28] answering service from his new apartment, he was told she had not picked up her messages[38] for over a month, and that as far as they were concerned, she had discontinued using their service. Bob,[5] as usual, wanted to leave his new number, but the service refused to accept any message[38] for Jane.[28] Bob[5] then went through her address book. Recognizing[52] the name of a man he had met at a dinner to which Clark had taken him, he called the man, who claimed not to remember[54] ever having met him. When Bob[5] mentioned Jane's[28] name, the man hung up. Borrowing some of the money he had found in Jane's[28] suitcase, Bob[5] went out and bought himself a suit. Then he picked a name from his own address book and called a couple he had met at Clark's house. They promptly invited him over for dinner that evening. On the way he stopped and bought a bottle of champagne. Six days later he called his parents in Princeton and informed them that he was getting married to someone he had met in the house of two close and dear friends of his. The wedding, they had decided, was to take place at the bride's parents' house in La Jolla. Bob[5] kept repeating that he hoped that they would make it to the wedding.

I just knew it, Bob's[5] father said exuberantly to his wife. The boy is a chip off the old block.

ZOO[76] / ZODIAC[77] / ZERO[78]

Bob[5] sent me a telegram inviting me to his wedding and then called me in New York to urge me to come. I hadn't seen him since he stayed at my place after giving up his apartment. On the phone he inquired jokingly if I was still a Mannix nut. It was he who had brought Jane[28] to my place a number of times. I told him how sorry I was to hear of her death, and he said, What? What? I guess no one reads the papers in L.A. All they do is fuck[18] around and go to the beach. How did she die, he asked. She was killed.[33] Shot,[56] I said. Apparently she moved around with a strange crowd. As far as I know, they haven't caught whoever did it. That's a shame, he said. I liked Jane.[28] I saw her only once. Only one time at the airport. But we'll talk about it when you[73] come out here for the wedding. You[73] will, won't you?[73] I miss you[73] an awful lot. I really didn't think you'd[73] get married, I said. She's very bright and attractive. She's got a Ph.D. in semiotics. Her father is in oil. When he hung up, I realized that he hadn't mentioned my latest book. The book is set in South California,[7] a place I've never visited. If not for Bob's[5] enthusiasm, I might not have undertaken[63] to write it.

READ-ONLY MEMORY

THE MESSENGER ABOUT-FACES

In the cradle of civilization men and women habitually sat face-to-face. They sat on stone benches or on the ground. The art of costume design was already well-advanced, although, I might add, these events preceded the invention of the doorknob and the windowpane. An abrupt about-face simply did not possess the impact it has today. No one was deadly wounded by it, and therefore it was not used as a weapon. Of course, just as today, people could not avoid bumping into each other on trails and out-of-the-way water holes. Who is to say that accident and not deliberate timing was the cause of those face-to-face encounters?

One hundred and seven years ago in New Mexico a woman named Jane Darway received an alarm clock from a distant admirer. In her time alarm clocks were not as common as they are today. What is he trying to tell me, mused Jane Darway as she unpacked the clock and stared at its black-and-white face. The hour hand pointed at the Roman numeral XII, the minute hand pointed at the Roman numeral XI. In those days most messages, even the dullest, were handwritten and delivered by hand. In a moment of great stress or inner turmoil a woman could always fall in a dead faint knowing that some hand would be around to revive her. This was something a distant admirer had to take into consideration. Whose hand would deliver his message. Would it be a repugnantly dirty hand. Jane Darway kept holding the messenger's hand. She had studied palmistry, philosophy, astronomy, and most of the sciences that proved so popular during the period of enlightenment. For years to come Jane Darway remembered the poignant encounter with the youthful messenger. She often thought of the power of the hand. Each evening before going to bed she would religiously wind the clock, but it never rang. One day Jane Darway passed away at the ripe old age of eighty-seven.

Our alarm clocks are implanted in our bodies. A middle-aged stockbroker I happen to know wears a hat of crushed velvet. He collects drawings of stout women wearing fur capes who limp. As far as he can see there is no actual need for a face-to-face encounter. He is a wealthy man, and it can be said that an entire industry was started on account of his somewhat spurious taste for crippled women. Some mothers subject their daughters to the most appalling tortures, hoping the investment will pay off. It's only a leg, a mother will tell her daughter. It's not as if you were going to climb Mount Everest next week.

No one has ever heard an alarm clock ring. Their presence is enough to cause alarm. Only people about-face. A messenger, having retrieved his perspiring hand, about-faces smartly; so does a firing squad after having riddled a man's chest and face with bullets. Even the man who gazes pensively at the yellow stream of his urine hitting the white enamel layer of the urinal will ultimately about-face. To do an about-face is to take one's leave. In an about-face the Chinese sent us their art treasures, not as a gesture of friendship or admiration, but simply because they did not wish to see them destroyed by our nuclear bombs.

Clearly, you're very prophetic, says Gwen to Harry as they discussed the Messianic symbolism in third-century Mosaic, a period known for its overwhelming despondency and sorrow. Do you mean B.C. or A.D., asks Harry. The United Parcel deliveryman who has just left is her husband. They now feel free to go to bed until five-thirty, when her husband returns. Gwen sets the clock and then undresses. Won't you about-face, says Harry.

THE MESSAGE IS ADEQUATE

The number of cars on the F train is considered adequate. During the early morning rush hour at least eight people are crushed each day. This number is considered tolerable. The following day the next of kin can pick up the morning paper and on the front page compare the accomplishments of their loved one to the accomplishments of the other victims. It has become common practice for the newspapers to embellish these accomplishments. For a slight remuneration the victim can receive a one-day posthumous honorary membership in the Yale or Princeton eating clubs. In a manner of speaking, the deceased's entire past now appears adequate. The reporters who cover the subway fatalities call it the "taste of death shift." Early each morning people fatalistically prepare themselves for another day at the office. Good-by table, they say as they leave their apartment. Good-by chair. Good-by, good-by. At that hour, the furniture seems adequate. They are quite prepared to live with it for another fifty years.

The people who disagree that the number of cars on the F train are adequate have been forced to go underground. They are said to exist as a movement. They have meetings at least once a week at which they discuss the minutes of the last meeting and what they intend to discuss at the next meeting. It is all very democratic. Now and then a new face is bloodied. People are expelled on procedural grounds. The movement is infiltrated by working-class agents of the subway system. As is always the case, the undercover agents are the most bellicose. If not for the undercover agents the meetings would be unbearably boring. The agents bring up the question of an adequate response to the daily death toll. So a few brick buildings in Queens are blown up. But it is done half-heartedly. Invariably someone fails to bring along the right fuse for the dynamite. Most of the buildings that are destroyed are orphanages and old age homes. There's always a great outcry following each incident, but behind closed doors city officials are smiling broadly. They have not studied statistics at NYU for nothing.

When Gwen first used the word "adequate," her husband had just purchased a second-hand convertible. Harry was invited to dinner. He was confused by Gwen's remark. Did she mean the fried liver, the convertible, United Parcel, her husband . . . or perhaps it was the fifty-nine-cent bouquet of marigolds Harry had picked up in the Port Authority. Adequate can be the grasp a person has on his past as well as his means of dealing with the future. A motorized army unit can be

considered just about adequate as it creeps along under fire not knowing where or when it will be able to refuel.

What are the means by which one can cling to an adequate life?
Well, there's always public housing; and then there are the public
baths. Two thousand light-years away an entire planet spent one-
third of its existence trying to duplicate a Viennese restaurant. It was
all done with the help of ESP. The restaurant, the size of Kentucky,
cost an arm and a leg. It was a really spectacular restaurant. The first
visitor from our planet to eat there would only say that the food was
adequate.

Our President's wife reads French novels in translation and dreams
of unexpected visitors to relieve the monotony of her life. She rarely
leaves her bed. At her feet lies her faithful poodle. Madame Bovary,
c'est moi, she said to Harry when he, searching for the men's room,
inadvertently entered her bedroom. Flustered, he tried to think of an
adequate response. Minutes pass, hours pass. What outrageous means
he was prepared to take in order not to plunder the reserves of his
fantasy.

AN APPOINTMENT TO RECEIVE THE MESSAGE

This is a return to the fantasy of time. This is a return to the over-
grown jungles and the stuffed leopards and the rich cuisine of turtle
and roasted mule. The male fantasy is filled with the rigorous need to
humiliate the Princess . . . to make her pick up the crown and fix the
sandwich: Ham and domestic Swiss, my love. Harry waits patiently
for his sandwich. Will she forget the lettuce? He also waits for the
letter that will cancel his appointment. In his spare time, like most
men, he subjugates naked women. Each day his calendar is filled with
fresh applicants.

I am not the man I used to be, thinks Harry. I was much more
broad-minded five years ago, before women began to publish their
candid if somewhat unrealistic accounts of their sexual encounters
with me. I am not the same man who felt so attached to Spider, my

pet crocodile. But all the same, Harry kept the leash in case Spider decided one day to return from the sewers. The difficulty in making any kind of appointment is that the buses do not run on time, and when people finally meet at lunch or supper, there is a note of disagreement in the air. Why am I seeing you again, is the unasked question. People seek out their differences . . . many stress these differences by arriving two hours late for an appointment. You didn't wait, they accuse the other when they meet again a year or two later. Is it any wonder that half the people, killing two hours by strolling in the park, are secretly devising means of getting rid of the other half asleep on the park benches.

On Thursday Harry has an appointment to meet two close friends of Gwen. He is meeting them at their hotel on Seventeenth and Lex. The men are called Humphrey and Jake. They are tough, soft-spoken men with slack jaws and large protruding bellies. They buy and sell rare stamps. The appointment, as Harry understood it, was extremely elastic. It could be changed or postponed. Both men are naked when Harry arrives two hours late. They have disagreeable bodies. The stamp albums are nowhere in evidence. I hope you don't mind, but we didn't wait, said Jake. Harry is in such a hurry to leave that he doesn't even bother to open the door as he makes his exit. Did you meet them, Gwen asked him when he went to see her. I've decided to choose another hobby, he said. Hobbies are nice, she said. I'll think of it, he replied.

Harry has an appointment with an English tailor. Ah, says the tailor, slyly inspecting Harry's wide seat. You must do a lot of riding. Now that you mention it, says Harry, I've always planned to take up riding.

Even riding stables require appointments. I have no ear for Mahler or Webern, says the stable boy, but that doesn't prevent me from indulging in the fantasy of the world's last cavalry charge.

The last charge? says Harry in surprise. There are certain things that he likes to hug to himself. There are certain things that he will not share with anyone else. This particular statement has struck his fancy. This particular statement is a case in point. It brings to mind a certain appealing pathos. The pathos of a certain absolutely predictable defeat. The pathos of a cavalry charge that is both futile and meaningless. Men armed only with swords or lances riding against a well-entrenched enemy armed with the latest automatic weapons.

You really mean what you say, asked Harry, as he mounted his horse.

What, asks the stable boy.

Riding in the last cavalry charge.

Don't bring it up, says the stable boy, unable to check the tears that were streaming down his cheeks.

It was quite common for people to weep in public in the Middle Ages. At least once a day large crowds gathered in the main square of the village and were moved to tears by the eloquent long-winded sermon of some traveling preacher who vividly depicted the horrors visited upon the innocent Christian mules by the horny and lecherous barbarians. That was a long time before riding stables became fashionable in the Bear Mountain area . . . and long before the Princess could be made to part with her precious memoirs, now available for twelve-ninety-five at your local bookstore.

Everyone is eager to read the memoirs . . . to catch a glimpse of the Princess when she was still undressing at parties, and using words like nifty and swell instead of *riffing*, a word that has now caught the popular imagination.

Harry found what he took to be the Princess's shoe on the Bowery. Close to tears he took it to his apartment and displayed it on a bookshelf next to Lefevre's *Everyday Life in the Modern World*. He vowed to himself that he would find the Princess . . . the poor limping Princess. He asked Gwen to try on the shoe, but it didn't fit; then he asked Jane to try on the shoe, but it didn't fit; then he asked Moira to try on the shoe, but it didn't fit . . . then he ran out of women to ask and began to ask men. On with the shoe, said a bartender at a Polish bar on the Bowery, and it fit. It's only a fucking shoe, said Harry to himself as he left the bar.

Are you ever going to grow up and stop playing childish games. Are you ever going to do something worthwhile with your life, demanded Jane. She had been waiting for him in his apartment. She had swept the floor and straightened his books. Are you going to keep accepting bedspread after bedspread from me, without feeling responsible for your actions? Are you simply going to hang your head everytime I speak to you . . . Harry drew the curtains over his eyes and fell asleep. Jane hobbled away on one shoe.

ACCESS

THE EMOTIONAL BARRIER

I don't see well in crowds, she explained. That is why I didn't greet
Harold. I didn't spot him. I didn't know that he had been invited.
I didn't expect to find him at a party for Terence and Cardinal. Now
he refuses to collect my garbage. He absolutely refuses to pick it up.
He stops the garbage truck in front of my house, picks up my next-
door neighbor's garbage, and then leaves. Harold is punctual. Every
second day at ten. The truck makes a great deal of noise. An intolerable
noise . . . I stay inside the house, the curtains drawn. I have explained
the misunderstanding to my neighbors. I can hear them chatting with
Harold . . . I have stopped going to cocktail parties.

The man who was crossing the lawn suddenly stopped. There was
no visible reason for him to do so. The people at the far end recognized him. He was someone they would see from time to time.
This, apparently, was to be one of those times. But he's stopped mid-
way, said Cardinal. He must have forgotten something, explained
Terence. He tends to forget things, and he's trying to decide whether
to return to his car or to come over. Perhaps we should wave to him,
said Margarete. No, said Cardinal, I wouldn't if I were you. It might
interfere with his reaching a decision.

I have forgotten something, the man said to himself. I have forgotten something that is vital and therefore must return to my car, looking absorbed, looking somewhat regretfully at the group assembled
on the terrace. Sorry, I'd love to come over and join you, but I've left
my glasses at home, and I had so much wanted to look at the titles of

all those books inside the library . . . Furthermore I don't really care
for crowded parties and coming late, and being introduced by Terence
and by Cardinal to all those people whose garbage I pick up.

Look who's out there, it's Harold, screamed Jean. Why is he standing
in the middle of our well-cut lawn.

AN ABSOLUTE BARRIER

Nothing whatever prevents Marks from entering the apartment building and taking the elevator to the fifth floor, and then quite casually
opening the door to his apartment. On the other hand, nothing would
have prevented him from sending Hilda a telegram as soon as he had
landed at Kennedy, to inform Hilda that he was back, and that at precisely eight o'clock he would open the door to their apartment. Naturally, the doorman recognizes him and holds open the door each time
he arrives or leaves. He walks to the elevator. The lobby of the building
is well lit. The building is well guarded, and he's confident that nothing
will be missing from their apartment. Just as he surmised, nothing is
missing. In the built-in closet hang his five new suits next to Hilda's
twenty-three new dresses. There is no barrier between them, and why
should there be? Even their toothbrushes frequently come in contact
with one another, and neither he nor Hilda recoil from dread or
loathing when this occurs. Hilda frequently uses the telephone to call
someone who is listed in the Manhattan telephone book. The telephone book is so to speak their common property. It also lists all the
people they haven't seen in years. It is tempting to call someone one
hasn't seen in years, simply to hear his voice, but they refrain from
doing so. As it is, their appointment books are filled with names and
numbers, and frequently the names and numbers in both their books
overlap. There is a certain pleasure to be taken from this overlapping.

In order to enter their apartment Marks has to insert his key in the
lock. He has done this a countless number of times without ever thinking about it. He has also countless times heard a key being inserted
in the lock while he happened to be inside the apartment. Invariably,
to his great pleasure and relief, it turned out to be Hilda and not
some stranger whose presence would pose a problem. In a way this
came as no surprise since Hilda, as far as he could determine, was the
only other person to possess a key to their apartment. She also had a
key to his car. Nothing is locked inside their apartment. Everything

inside the apartment lies there, open to be seen, to be looked at by either one or the other. His diary, her notes, his letters, her messages. Both use the electric typewriter and the portable typewriter and the adding machine and one of the dozen pencils that are in a Fortnum & Mason jar, which once contained Finest English Stilton Cheese, to jot down their feelings. They also get up in the middle of the night, sometimes in the middle of making love, excuse themselves, and then hastily scribble on a piece of paper exactly how they feel at that particular moment. These feelings are not written down in order to be kept from the other, no, they are pursued because both Marks and Hilda consider them elusive. Both take a certain pleasure in capturing their feelings, although they agree that no one knows what they are feeling at any precise moment because feelings are evanescent and bound to change, or to be erroneous, or misleading . . .

Hilda has a brand-new sewing machine, and when Marks is away on business she will sit down at her sewing machine and sew a new dress. Each time he is gone for several days a new dress appears in the closet. Nothing much is ever said about it. He takes her skill pretty much for granted. Naturally he admires the dress and says: fantastic, and now how about a quick lamb chop, or words to that effect. The key to the apartment can easily be duplicated at any hardware store, and the notes they so frequently jot down can be copied by any Xerox machine. The ability to duplicate everything they possess fills a great and useful need. It also frees them of a certain amount of worry. For instance: What will I do if I lose my key or misplace my most recent notation. The keys also act as a kind of identifying marker. He carries a few keys in his pocket. He knows the key for each lock. He has seen Hilda's key chain . . . and counted her keys, twenty-three keys at the latest count. That is a lot of keys, he said to himself, raising one eyebrow. A lot of keys for one key chain . . .

He came home unexpectedly and let himself into the apartment. It was spotlessly clean. Although he had come home a day sooner than he said he would, nothing, absolutely nothing was out of place. He took a shower, made himself a chicken sandwich, and then leisurely examined the twenty-fourth dress in the closet.

THE PHYSICAL BARRIER

Terence and Cardinal had flown in from Washington. They did not know the city, but the familiar components that constitute a city out-

weighed the uncertainty posed by the unfamiliar topography. Both·
Terence and Cardinal spoke a language that was instantly understood
by the cab driver. Being understood cheered them up considerably.
It confirmed the wisdom of their decision to come and see me. Actually
there was no need for them to see me in person. They could have
conducted their business on the phone. They could have told me
exactly what kind of material they had in mind for the textbook.
They could have put the list of words that I was not to use in the mail.
A German, Italian, Korean, and Vietnamese edition are to follow the
publication of the English text. In time, Terence confided, Washington
envisions worldwide distribution to all school systems here and abroad.
The subject of the text book is how we live. It'll be a cheerful book,
because the people in Washington insisted that it be a cheerful book.
It is to make us a lot of friends among the twelve- to fifteen-year-olds.
I nodded in agreement. I was eager to proceed with the job. I had
begun to do the required research, I explained somewhat ingratiat-
ingly, and by now could churn out 100,000 words without difficulty.
Needless to say there are all kinds of difficulties. For one thing, I have
been without water for eight days due to a broken water pipe in
the building; a further annoyance is the unaccountable animosity of
the plumbers who, it seems to me, are deliberately prolonging my dis-
comfort. Furthermore, I cannot possibly invite Terence or Cardinal to
my place, because my place might give them the wrong impression. It
might prove to be too cheerless, too cluttered and untidy for someone
who is about to undertake the task of writing a textbook about the way
we live. I was sorry that on the list they handed me of words that
were not to be used in any circumstance was the word barrier . . .
My fondness for the word barrier has nothing to do with it. Barriers
are part of our everyday life. We are cheerful when we avoid the
barriers placed in our path. I don't know the Japanese or Vietnamese
word for barrier. I must admit that in the past my stubborn attach-
ment to certain words, words that were no longer found to be appropriate, had cost me numerous well-paying commissions. Yes, one pays
a price for clinging to words that have lost their significance. Still, it's
a small price. I've been cutting down on meals for the sake of words.
One frankfurter on a roll in Zum Zum, a chain of restaurants with
white tiles on the walls and German waitresses, will hold me until
supper.

I could see at once that Terence and Cardinal had come to New
York with a certain expectation, an expectation they did not bother to

hide from me. Their expectation encompasses the porno films and possibly a little dingdong under the covers. It is only to be expected. I do what I can to encourage their expectations. Something more than Zum Zum is called for. Fortunately there is an expensive restaurant on the ground floor of the hotel where they are staying. We pick a nice table with a view of the park. How we live, says Terence jokingly as I choose the filet mignon. A textbook existence, I reply. We laugh. They're really not a bad bunch once you get to speak their language. Halfway through the filet mignon I spot Hilda at the next table. She is sipping a cocktail. She is eying us. Hilda, the wife of my best friend, Marks. I wave to her. Terence and Cardinal look at me expectantly. I'll be glad to introduce you, I say and walk over to Hilda. Hi Hilda, I was thinking of you only yesterday. Marks is out of town, says Hilda. Whenever he's out of town I come here for a drink . . . I like the decor. Care to join us, I ask. Seated at my table are Terence and Cardinal, and they would like to meet you. The ground felt firm under my legs as Hilda smiled at Terence and Cardinal. They both had ordered something simple, something that would not prove too difficult for the chef. Now they look extremely alert as Hilda smiles. They both stand up, having decided that Hilda's smile is not a barrier. Hilda's husband, I explain, is in textiles. He travels a lot. Lovely fellow . . . good outdoorsman . . . great shot . . . How do you like my new dress, asks Hilda.

Later, following coffee and dessert, we took the elevator to the eighth floor. It's so funny running into you today, I said to Hilda. I had been thinking of you for the past few days. The buttons are numbered from one to twenty on the aluminum panel in the elevator. We pressed eight and watched it light up. In addition to the numbered buttons, there were others marked HOLD, CLOSE, PH for penthouse, and B for basement. No guest in his right mind would ever press the button marked B. B to anyone acquainted with the city also stood for Barrier, and what more likely place to find one than in the basement.

When the elevator door slid open we all peered out. There was a bronze plaque on the wall facing us with the numeral eight. But could we rely on it? Hilda is wearing a bright sleeveless number made of rayon. She is also carrying a rather smart but bulky handbag. Neither Terence nor Cardinal who keep eyeing the bag have yet reached any conclusion as to what it may contain. It was large enough to demolish the brightness of their evening. Unlike me both of them wore starched white shirts. No one would mistake them for members of an excavating crew. They looked like grim businessmen engaged in a familiar pursuit. Both were hopefully regarding Hilda's face and trying to read what the face said, and what it didn't say. Being businessmen they were a bit hesitant to jump to any conclusions regarding her availability, and consequently somewhat hesitant as to how to proceed. My name is Hilda, said Hilda, and I have a friend who is staying in 1804. She volunteered this information as soon as we had reached their room. Terence and Cardinal exchanged quick glances. 1804 entailed another trip filled with all kinds of risks, but they decided, what the hell . . . Her name is Martha, said Hilda, and on weekdays she runs a nifty little boutique on Lexington Av. Had I ever met her, I wondered as we took the elevator to the eighteenth floor. 1804 proved to be identical to the room we had just left. It contained twin beds, a color TV, a built-in closet, a white shag carpet, reading lamps on a small cabinet at the side of each bed, a view of New Jersey, and a reproduction of *The Artillerymen* by Rousseau. I peered into the bathroom. A quick glance at the white tiles on the wall. The white tiles of my childhood happiness. Would Martha object if I took a shower. It's been eight days since I had a shower. Martha wore a pair of tight-fitting trousers. Her smile, if anything, was a trifle more practiced than Hilda's. Both Terence and Cardinal must have found it disconcerting since they gripped their brief cases more tightly. They were on their guard. Martha's smile filled them with a vague foreboding. They had encountered a similar smile before. Make yourself at home, said Hilda. Martha mixed them a drink. She said she did not mind if I took a shower. Bless your heart, I said.

Drink in one hand, briefcase in the other, Terence and Cardinal stood at the window staring at New Jersey and making appropriate remarks. New Jersey brings out the worst in people . . . it also unites them. Make yourself at home, said Hilda. We feel at home here, said Cardinal, gingerly sitting down on one of the twin beds, still gripping his briefcase. He could hear me humming in the bathroom. Possibly my unexpected action had put him on his guard, since, as we all know, the pleasant and overwhelmingly familiar can often conceal a deadly barrier. The only barrier between me and my happiness, reflected Hilda, is my past. But the past is no barrier to what I intend to do now. When she undressed and then, naked, crouched on the white shag carpet, it was not done at the suggestion of either Terence or Cardinal. She did so because by crouching she could best over-come any barrier that might suddenly be thrust in front of her. Bar-riers impede one's initiative. Terence stared helplessly at Cardinal, both being at a loss on what to do. They stared at Hilda, then they stared at her friend Martha, then back at Hilda, as if she had by this incom-prehensible act become a barrier . . . was she blocking their exit . . . Just give her time, said Martha. Her husband is in textiles, and their rent has been raised to four-fifty a month. Now they are also behind in their car payments. This information enabled the men to relax some-what . . . they looked more closely at Hilda . . . she did have splen-did legs and a most attractive figure . . . but her unexpected action made it incumbent upon them to respond. It's fifty each, explained Martha. Fifty bucks? Now they were really confused. Where had I led them. They could feel a certain stiffness in their arms and legs. It must be the drink, Terence decided . . . it must be something in the drink that was causing this unusual stiffness.

How do I know that this actually took place while I was taking a prolonged shower. I know it because Hilda told me everything, every detail . . . I listened calmly, surprised that it didn't hurt . . . Hilda, the wife of my best friend. When I raced down to the eighth floor an hour later, Terence and Cardinal had checked out. I wonder if there's a message for me, I asked the desk clerk. No, said the clerk. In that case, I decided, I might as well take the elevator back to the eighteenth floor. Later, toward evening, I stopped at Zum Zum for a frankfurter. I wasn't hungry, but I thought it would be nice for a change to hear someone speak a foreign language, a language I didn't understand.

THE ACQUISITION BARRIER

Hilda stopped in front of the store window and examined each article that was on display. It was a chic little store, and each article in the window was arranged in such a way as to express both the impeccable taste of the owner as well as the luxurious quality of the article itself. When Hilda peeked into the store she caught a glimpse of a young woman waiting on a customer. The woman behind the counter resem-bled Hilda. She was a few years younger, but there was, it seemed to Hilda, an unmistakable resemblance. Entering the store, Hilda asked the young woman if she was the one who had arranged the window. Yes, said the woman. Are you also, by any chance, the woman who places the orders for all these beautiful dresses. Yes, said the woman. Then you must be the owner. Yes, said the woman, but I have a silent partner who helps with the bookkeeping. I've always wanted to own a little store like this, commented Hilda wistfully.

Every few days from then on Hilda would drop in and buy something she did not really need. She bought a lot of silk scarves and blouses and gloves and an umbrella only in order to have an opportunity to speak to the young woman who was running the store . . . In time the woman came to know Hilda's name, and where Hilda lived, and what Hilda did with her time. She would also save a special scarf or a blouse for Hilda, knowing that Hilda would like it.

You aren't married, are you? Hilda asked the woman. No, she said. Hilda was dying to ask more questions, especially about the silent partner, but it was too soon. She had not been a customer long enough. Another few weeks perhaps, and further questions could safely be asked.

THE LANGUAGE BARRIER

Language is not a barrier. Language enables people in all circumstances to cope with a changing world; it also permits them to engage in all sorts of activities without unduly antagonizing everyone in their immediate vicinity. Language also makes it easier on the man and woman who wish after years of separation to come together. Clearly, without language this would be a next to impossible task. Furthermore, language allows one to express a renewed interest in an object, a hobby, or a person, an interest that may admittedly be only a pretext for yet another and greater need.

I'm not really concerned with language. As a writer I'm principally concerned with meaning. What, for instance, does being a writer mean in the context of this society. For one thing, in this society, it is almost taken for granted that a writer, irrespective of sex, irrespective of age, irrespective of political conviction, irrespective of wealth or geographic location, will use the language spoken by the majority of the people in this country. He will be using the words that fill their days and nights with unbearable tension and dread. In that respect, writers perform a vital task, they resuscitate words that are about to be obliterated by a kind of willful negligence and general boredom. Writers frequently are able to inject a fresh meaning into a word and thereby revitalize the brain cells of the reader by feeding the brain information it does not really require. For instance, I have recently revitalized a couple of million brain cells by referring to barriers. Barriers appear in my writings more frequently than they deserve. It is now on its way to becoming a new word again. I feel there is a barrier between us, a man can once again tell a woman and be understood. The statement clearly is intended to have a slightly menacing effect. It is also intended to convey a threat: Shape up you bitch, or I'll sock you in the mouth . . . Women, as always, respond by trying to find the barrier, blaming themselves, their nearsightedness, their bad cooking, for its existence.

On Tuesday I receive a call from Marks. Hilda has left him. She's moved in with a friend who runs a boutique on Lexington Av. I know her, I said. Her name is Martha. No, said Marks. Not any more. She's just changed her name to Paul.

IN SO MANY WORDS

60

admires also America and apartment back bare be better between blue buildings can casual city elegant elongated exists extremely eyes far feet forth green identifiable immediately in instance is it large larger map mind note of on over parquet permit relationship replicating roving shape shining square stretched tall terrain that the this those to uncluttered underside unimpeded unspoiled wander windows

93

America is extremely fond of the casual relationship that exists between the underside of the bare feet and the shining parquet floor. It also admires the large windows (the larger the better) that permit the roving blue (note the blue) eyes to wander unimpeded back and forth over the uncluttered, unspoiled terrain, the terrain in this instance is also immediately identifiable on the map of the city, the elongated green square shape on the map replicating, if the mind can be stretched that far, the elongated windows on those tall elegant apartment buildings.

34

also America American are as brains but city come etc. every imprinted in institutions like live major mapped not of one only other outlines parks people si.eets the this to visit well who work

43

Like every other American city in America, the outlines of this one, as well as the major streets, institutions, parks, etc., are not only mapped but also imprinted on the brains of the people who live, work, or come to visit the city.

74

32
*a an and at Bendel brain building coexists deep forth has her houses in
into is like lives location looking map of office park peering she so that
the where with which*
47
In her brain the location of the park coexists with the building where
she lives, and the building in which she has an office, and the building
that houses Bendel, and so forth. Looking at a map of the city is like
peering deep into the brain.
40
*a absolutely and at America American building certain convulsed
croissant delicious eighth elongated floor four from height her in intended irony is it Lee munching no of one perfection perspective quite
Sara she splendor standing taking the true windows with*
48
Standing at one of the elongated windows, munching a Sara Lee croissant (quite delicious) she is taking in the American perfection, the
American splendor—absolutely no irony intended. It is true. From a
certain height and perspective, the eighth floor of her building, America is convulsed with perfection.
48
*a actually American and beasts below but city dogs dream eat few
get go herd hoofbeats horses magnificent moment Nevada not occasionally of only open out people purebred snatch solitude spread taste
terrain that the their them this those thundering to uninterrupted unspoiled vistas walk where wild yes*
69
Spread out below is the unspoiled terrain where the city people go to
snatch a few moments of uninterrupted solitude and dream of the
thundering hoofbeats of the herd, the open vistas, the wild horses of
Nevada. Yes, this is where the city people dream and walk their magnificent purebred dogs, those American beasts that not only dream of
the wild horses but occasionally actually get to taste them.
40
*absorbing acutely akin all American and ant are aware constitute criss-
crossing dressing each foot framework gown her horse in individuals
movement of on other outdoor people perfection tall terrain that the
they setting she sized something stands who window within*
53
She stands in her dressing gown absorbing the movement of the people

who are crisscrossing the terrain, on foot, on horse, acutely aware that they and all the other ant sized individuals constitute within the framework of each tall window something akin to perfection, the perfection of an outdoor setting . . . the American perfection.

43

a Abercrombie able also and barefoot binoculars but by cheeks drawbacks easily eighth enhanced exterior Fitch floor freshly from her if interior is it male minor of on only parquet perfection rectified riders see shaven she standing that the to unable use were

57

Is she also aware that by standing barefoot on her parquet floor the exterior perfection is enhanced by the interior perfection. From the eighth floor she is unable to see the freshly shaven cheeks of the male riders, but it is only a minor drawback, easily rectified if she were to use her Abercrombie and Fitch binoculars.

58

a against all America American are be cards cigarettes cheeks coffee chrome deck dreamily expensive fence fond freshly general glass glossy heavy horseback in into is its large lazy leaning like magazine men of on opulence or out pages perching reproduced rock shaven smoking smooth some space spread staring table tall that the thick those to who

76

America, in general, is fond of the smooth freshly shaven cheeks of the tall men who are to be found on horseback or lazily leaning against some large rock or perching on a fence, smoking a cigarette, staring dreamily into the American space that is reproduced in all its opulence on the pages of those thick glossy magazines that like a deck of cards are spread out on the heavy expensive chrome and glass coffee table.

26

also America American and are by fond Gillette good is made manufacturers more name names of popular products razor safety Schick solid the they to two

34

America is also fond of the safety razor made by Gillette and Schick, to name two of the more popular manufacturers. Gillette and Schick are American products. They are also good solid American names.

19

a an Gillette her in introduction is legs morning once razor safety shave she that the this uses week

22

This is an introduction to the Gillette safety razor that she uses to shave her legs once a week in the morning.

41

a an and as available color colors compulsions daily dark dozen dread drugstores everyone's handle in inexpensive is it lies many men model most of on open popular prefer razor safety sell somber the their to two unbreakable variety whole

58

The safety razor lies open to everyone's view. It is an inexpensive model. It is unbreakable. It is a popular model and drugstores sell as many as two dozen daily. The handle is available in a variety of colors. On the whole, most men prefer dark colors, the somber colors, the color of their dark compulsion and dread.

35

a acquired and as at attention bathtub bending blade down entire firmly focused fresh gripped handle heightened her inserted ledge leg legs on peering proceeded propping shave she significance slightly the them time to yellow

44

She firmly gripped the yellow handle, inserted a fresh blade, and proceeded to shave her legs. Propping one leg at a time on the bathtub ledge, bending slightly, peering down, her legs acquired a heightened significance as she focused her entire attention on them.

96

a acquaintance ads aglow American and another are assistance before begin breakfast cannot cereal cheeks cigarette Crack Crackle Crunch day encircled envy even evening faces for foreigners generally Gillette goes good gripped habit have health hearty heavy her horse how image in instead is it kick legs long men must next no of on one or packs park place pose preference really ride Schick shave shaved she shortly show slim solid smokers sometimes soon spitting stunning tall telling that the their there they this those to took two usually visit want well when who will with yes

130

This generally took place shortly before breakfast. Sometimes it took place in the evening. There is no telling when she will next shave her legs. Those stunning long slim legs that have gripped and encircled the spitting image of those tall men who pose for cigarette ads. Yes, her legs are well acquainted with those heavy cigarette smokers who can-

not kick the two packs a day and ride a horse in the park before breakfast habit. America really goes for the hearty breakfast. Even foreigners on a visit soon begin to show their preference for one cereal instead of another. They want Crack Crackle instead of Crackle Crunch.
How they must envy those good solid American faces, cheeks aglow
with health, cheeks shaved with the assistance of Gillette or Schick.

61

*a and anyhow as at away bathtub been but by cars clean comes daily
for had have her hurry in intensity it ledge left love lying men must
nine not of office on placed polish proper put razor repository safety
same she show shiny somewhat that the their then they to up was
weekend where white will wipe with woman*

84

By nine she was at her office, the safety razor left lying where she had
placed it on the white shiny ledge of the bathtub. The bathtub was
not the proper repository for the safety razor, but she must have been
in somewhat of a hurry. Anyhow, the woman who comes to clean up
daily will put it away and then wipe the ledge with the same love and
intensity that men show as they clean and polish their cars on the
weekend.

36

*and at bare bathtub discern dry fabricate feet gaze go her imprint
ledge leg naked narrow occasional of on one only other rest shiny so
speak standing that the to toilet using visitor will with yet*

52

Will the occasional visitor using the toilet gaze at the bathtub ledge
and discern the imprint of her bare feet, and then, with only that to go
on, fabricate, so to speak, the rest of her standing naked on one leg, the
other on the narrow ledge, the shiny yet dry ledge.

4

an incredible surface what

4

What an incredible surface.

2

incredible whiteness

2

Incredible whiteness.

4

of perfection the whiteness

4
The whiteness of perfection.
16
admonition bear by even is indefinite perfection repetition she tedium the troubled not of will Whitehead's
16
Is she troubled by Whitehead's admonition: "Even perfection will not bear the tedium of indefinite repetition."
39
a adventure again although ardor brown but civilization costume essential first for intensity is it its learning light more morning namely new not of perfect perfection require search she sustains than the this to was white Whitehead with wore
46
This morning she wore a costume again. Although the costume was not white but a light brown, it was perfect. Whitehead again: "To sustain a civilization with the intensity of its first ardor requires more than learning. Adventure is essential, namely, the search for new perfections."
2
bathtubs new
2
New bathtubs.
31
ageless American apartment bring claim cleaning cleans enough every grain have her in ingredient is known lays object of old out polishes precious scrubs she surfaces that the to Whitehead woman
40
The cleaning woman is ageless. She polishes, scrubs, cleans to bring out the American grain, that precious ingredient that lays claim to the surface of every object in her apartment. The cleaning woman is old enough to have known Whitehead.
38
a an and artichokes bacon been Boston cereal chicken cigarettes cleaning coffee croissant Draino eggs envelope for frozen has in is Lee left lettuce list margarine money mushrooms next one peas Sara shopping soap spinach the to woman
43
The money for the cleaning woman has been left in an envelope. Next

to the envelope is a shopping list. Eggs, coffee, bacon, cereal, mushrooms, Boston lettuce, Sara Lee croissants, artichokes, frozen peas, frozen spinach, one chicken, soap, margarine, cigarettes, and Draino.
41
a an anyone at aware bar boy did doorman driver elevator evening for freshly friend gloves had he her him his later legs man met neighborhood not of office old other plans shaven she tax the up was wearing white wondered
53
Was anyone aware of her freshly shaven legs, she wondered? Was the elevator man, the doorman wearing his white gloves, the taxi driver, the office boy, the man she met later at a neighborhood bar? He was an old friend. She did not invite him up. She had other plans for the evening.
24
admired although am an as costume did flat freshly friend hairdo her I invite legs me nasal not old shaven she up voice well
28
I am an old friend as well. She did not invite me up, although I admired her costume, her hairdo, her flat nasal voice, her freshly shaven legs.
43
a accustomed American an at briefly degree disappointed dry easily element every familiar firm go grip hand held how I in it let may meeting my not of perfection possess possession possessive quickly relinquished taking that thing to she some upon was would
62
Briefly, upon meeting, she held my hand in a firm grip. A dry possessive grip. A familiar grip. A grip that was accustomed to taking possession of every thing that may to some degree possess an element of perfection. It was a grip that would not easily let go. An American grip. I was disappointed at how quickly she relinquished my hand.
30
above all America America's and any are aroma cheeks fear had have her I into it legs limp many may men's not of perspiration prick running the unfounded unshaven were
41
Any fears I may have had of running into her were unfounded. America's fears are not unfounded. America fears the unshaven legs, the un-

shaven men's cheeks, the aroma of perspiration, and the limp prick. Above all it fears the limp prick.

41

a America America's American ardor be by can civilization clearly fear first good he how in intensity is its keeps learning limp mind more name of old paranoia prick referring requires states sustain sustained than that the to when Whitehead wishing

53

America keeps Whitehead in mind. Whitehead is a good old American name. When Whitehead states that a civilization wishing to sustain the intensity of its first ardor requires more than learning, he is clearly referring to America's paranoia, the fear of the limp prick. How can ardor be sustained by a limp prick?

22

America America's and assistance do electric have how industries it limp of prick produced razor revive safety that the toothbrush will with

29

How will America revive the limp prick? It will do it with the assistance of America's industries, the industries that have produced the safety razor and the electric toothbrush.

129

a action adventure alike also American and appearance are as astonishing at belief beyond black bland blue braided brass bulging but cap clean closer construction couple crotch Dad daily design differed disfigured doing each eight elevator examination exceptionally faces father floor foreign found from God good had hair haired have handkerchiefs he heavy his I if in into is it jackets jeans leather like lips looked looks man men must my noses nostrils not nothing number obscene of off old on operation or ornate other our pants perfect perfectly picture please proposals protruding puckered queers rose said scribble slightly small specifically stain stains stared staring stepped still stood the three town troubled unanimously uniform urinate walls was way were what white Whitehead who will with wondered would yellow zippers

234

Whitehead would have found nothing astonishing or exceptionally adventurous in the action of the three men who stepped into the elevator and said, eight please. The construction of the elevator and the number eight were not foreign to Whitehead. But the three men were foreign to the white haired elevator operator. He was troubled by their appearance. Specifically by their black leather jackets. The jackets looked alike, but on closer examination differed in design from each other. All had heavy brass zippers. The elevator man was also troubled by their bland small town faces . . . by those puckered lips and slightly disfigured noses. What are they doing in my elevator, he wondered? If they had their way with this elevator they would scribble their obscene proposals on the walls, and then, to cap it off, they would urinate on the floor. A stream of yellow will stain the floor I clean daily. The crotch of their blue jeans is bulging beyond belief, thought the elevator man. They must have stuffed a couple of handkerchiefs into their pants. Those bloody queers. The three men stood staring at the old man. They stared at his braided cap, his ornate uniform, and at the stains on the ornate uniform, and at the white hair protruding from his nostrils . . . Good God, they thought unanimously. He looks like Dad. Our Dad. The picture of an American father. The perfect Dad.

48

American an and as bedroom bliss counting distance divides eight 8 extension 5 flat floor 4 grip had her horizontal in is joy line lips meantime of 1 pacing prairie pride 7 she 6 soon steps takes that the then thin 3 toward turns 2 was will window

71

In the meantime she was pacing the floor. The flat thin horizontal line that divides her thin lips is an extension of the distant horizon line in the prairie. She is counting, 1, 2, 3, 4, 5, 6, 7, 8, as she takes eight steps toward the window, then turns and takes eight steps toward the bedroom . . . Soon her hands will grip the American joy, the American bliss, the American pride.

60

a after am American amiable an and are barstool bartender bring by class crack cracks democratization exchange first from Gillette greetings hands his I in introduction is it jacket knuckles left moist moment of on person pick Schick serve sitting sound spot suddenly surprise table takes the there third this tip to together we white wipe working up us yet

83

This is an introduction to the first person. I am sitting on the third barstool from the left. We exchange greetings. The amiable bartender in his white jacket suddenly cracks his knuckles. It takes us by surprise. Crack, crack, crack, the sound of American working class knuckles. The hands are there to serve us, to wipe up after us, to pick up the tip left on a moist spot on the table. Yet Gillette and Schick bring us together . . . a moment of democratization.

42

a all also and are bartender bartender's by cheeks design do each examine face fail for his I identical in is know knuckles longer morning my no not of one quarter razor safety she six smooth that the to use used uses

53

Each morning I use a safety razor that is identical in design to the one she uses, and for all I know, to the one used by the bartender. By quarter of six my cheeks are no longer smooth. I examine the bartender's face . . . I also do not fail to examine his knuckles.

20

a and body cake gently her I large legs mine of once same shave she soap soaped the using watched

30

Once I watched her shave her legs. Using a large cake of soap she gently soaped her legs. Using the same cake of soap she soaped her body and mine.

99

a actually also American an and apartment at barefoot Bendel blouse bought briefly buy by called car comes crash day dear deity doing dollar earrings ecstasy entire exotic familiar feelings feet fifty floor foot for four frequently friend from gallery grow has have height her hundred I in intended is it jade leaving mind moment natives of office on only overcome pair parquet perfect perfection personifies place plant pray presently print rainforest reaches Rosenquist seven she sheer spent spot spur standing stood Sumatra tall that the there three to told until uptown very visit was weekend what whom will

169

She spent the entire day at the office, leaving it only briefly to buy a Rosenquist print of a car crash at an uptown gallery, a blouse at Bendel, and a pair of jade earrings for a dear friend she intended to visit that weekend. She also, on the spur of the moment, bought an exotic plant. The plant is presently four feet tall. It comes from the rainforest of Sumatra. It will grow and grow until it reaches the height of seven foot three. In Sumatra the natives pray to the plant, she is told. The plant personifies a deity, and in Sumatra it is called perfection. She has the perfect place for it in the apartment. I have frequently stood on the very spot she has in mind. It is the perfect place for a three hundred and fifty dollar plant. Actually, what was I doing, standing there? I was standing barefoot on her parquet floor overcome by the familiar American feeling, the feeling of sheer ecstasy.

53

a above achievement acknowledged all also America and applause approbation ardor be bravery control dexterity each expects everything for fucks general gifts give he herself his honesty in incredible inventiveness is kind like loves man of passion people plant recognition reward rewards self-control some stamina the their themselves time to women would yes

73

The plant is a gift to herself. Daily people give themselves gifts in recognition of their honesty, bravery, and self-control. America loves gifts. All gifts. America also loves rewards, recognition, applause, ardor, passion, and general approbation. Each time a man fucks a woman he expects some kind of reward for his incredible achievement, his stamina, his ardor, inventiveness, dexterity, and control . . . yes, above everything he would like his self-control to be acknowledged.

34

a and away boats bundle cars everyone expensive fucked giving her houses I liberally made one opera pajamas practiced ranches reward rings self-control she shirts the tickets tidy ties time to used watches who

37

At one time she used to reward liberally everyone who fucked her, giving away expensive ties, shirts, pajamas, rings, watches, cars, houses, ranches, and tickets to the opera. I practiced at self-control and made a tidy bundle.

38

a advised although American an and at bought broken Commonwealth competent complaining fucking gamely George have he I I'll I'm it keep low me not of oil password preferred said shares the try 24,000 2¼ unusual up was

46

I'm not complaining. I have a competent broker. Keep it up, he advised me. It was the American password. Keep it up. I'll try, I said gamely, although I preferred fucking George. I'll try, and bought 24,000 shares of Commonwealth Oil at an unusual low, 2¼.

44

and any around at bathroom come day did doing doorman down ele-
vator furniture her hoods in indescribable leave men messing might
moment neither night not operator or razors see slightly still that the
them there they things three to unspeakable up were wielding worried

63

The night doorman did not see the three men leave, neither did the
day doorman, neither did the day or night elevator operator. It worried them slightly to see her leave, knowing that the three hoods were
still up there, messing around, doing indescribable things to the furniture, doing unspeakable things in the bathroom. They might come
down at any moment wielding razors.

85

a all an and another armpits at attention avoid bar behind breakfast
bright but calls car costume costumes dark demanded desk did down-
ward drink driver few for friend from glanced glasses good had hardly
have her him home in into invite life looking making morning neigh-
borhood never not of office old once other out place plans pretend ran
rapid receiving regular sat seen shaved she shower some someone
spotted spring stopped strokes tax the to told took tried unobserved up
was went windows with wore

135

She shaved her armpits with rapid downward regular strokes. She
was unobserved. She took a shower, had breakfast, and went to her
office. A bright spring morning. She sat behind her desk receiving a
few calls, making a few calls. Some calls demanded all her attention.
She wore another costume. She looked good in costumes, someone had
once told her. She took a taxi home from the office. She had never
seen the driver before in her life. She wore her dark glasses and hardly
glanced out of the car window. She stopped for a drink at the neighborhood bar and ran into an old friend. She tried to avoid him, to pretend not to have seen him, but he spotted her. She did not invite him
up to her place. She had other plans.

42

a an and anything as black designed elevator especially for her in in-
corporated into introduction is it jackets leather left men moment no
of on one operator other plans rose said sank shaft stepped stood that
the this three to use within

52

This is an introduction to the other plans. The plans incorporated the use of the elevator that rose and sank within a shaft especially designed for it. The operator stood on the left as the three men in black leather jackets stepped into the elevator. For a moment no one said anything.

10

admitted doorman elevator informed man men that the three were

12

The elevator man informed the doorman that the three men were admitted.

65

and apartment arrived at back be broken cleaning come company darned defaced disappointed door doorman elevator empty for from front furniture gone had have he hoods I'll Irma man may not nothing of opened operator out place report room said seemed she sounding ten that the their then to until unwelcome upstairs waited waiting walls wangs was wasn't watch well were when with woman you

84

Watch out, Irma, said the doorman to the cleaning woman when she arrived at ten. You may have unwelcome company waiting for you upstairs with their wangs out. The elevator man waited until Irma had opened the front door and then waited and waited until she had gone from room to room and come back to report that the apartment was empty. The walls were not defaced, the furniture wasn't broken, nothing seemed out of place. Well, I'll be darned, he said, sounding disappointed.

124

a after alike all almost although always an and another answer answering anxiety as ask at barely be behind brought but buttons cab call callousness carefully closet coffee communication costumes could depend desk did disagreeable downpour dozen due ear eight even eyebrows exuded faint find frequently had hanging her hour if in indifference inquiry insecurity instantly invite it juice left lift line lips long mahogany make many marmalade morning need never not occasionally occur of office on one or orange parted plucked pressed put receiver respects sat say secretary secretary's selected selection share she shower similar simply slice so sound take telephone that the their thin three time to toast together toneless two very voice was went were. when white with world would yes

217

She carefully plucked her eyebrows in the morning. Plucked them as

if she had all the time in the world. She had a slice of toast with marmalade, orange juice, and coffee after her shower. She selected one of
the two or three dozen costumes hanging in her closet. The selection
did not take very long. In many respects, all the costumes were so similar, so alike. She went to the office. She sat behind her mahogany
desk. Occasionally she would lift the receiver of her telephone and answer a call or make one. When answering a call, she would simply say,
yes. The yes, a flat and almost toneless sound, was an inquiry, a line of
communication that barely parted her thin lips. The white telephone had eight buttons. One of the buttons, when pressed, instantly brought to her ear the faint anxiety in her secretary's voice. She
did not find the anxiety and insecurity her secretary exuded at all disagreeable. She could depend on her secretary. She could always ask
her to put in another hour if need be. Although she frequently left together with her secretary, it would never, not even in a downpour, occur to her to invite her secretary to share her cab. It was not due to
callousness, but simply indifference.

37

against appearances are aware bear but contrary despite did even ever
filled herself I'm indefinite lives manages nevertheless not nothing of
our perfection properly quite repetition same she shield stated tedium
that the to Whitehead will with

47

Quite properly, Whitehead stated that even perfection will not bear
the tedium of indefinite repetition. I'm aware that our lives are filled
with repetition. Nevertheless, she manages, despite appearances to the
contrary, to shield herself against the familiar. To her, nothing she did
seemed ever the same.

88

a after although an and another around astounded at back bar barman
be before brain chose clipped completely corner cut did difficult drink
driver elevator entered exactly five fragility fragments frugally glanced
glass going goodbye greeting grip hailed hand handkerchief happened
has he held her his ignorant in informed interested it latter lobby
long me meter might miss neck next Slavic sweet table taken taxi
testing the then thoughts through tipped to told took unusual up voice
walked was watched what when where window wipe wished without
wrapped

177

At five she took the elevator to the lobby. She did not see the other people in the elevator. She walked to the corner and hailed a taxi. She informed the driver in her clipped voice where exactly she wished to be taken. She was completely ignorant of what might be going through his brain . . . she was not interested in his thoughts, in his long Slavic name, or in the back of his neck. She glanced at the meter. She tipped frugally. She entered the bar without greeting me, although it was difficult to miss seeing me. She chose a table next to a window. She ordered one drink then another. She held the glass in a surprisingly strong grip. She was testing the fragility, the perfection of glass, astounded when it shattered in her hand. It was not an unusual occurrence, the barman told me later. She wrapped a handkerchief around her cut palm and watched the barman wipe the table after he had swept up the glass fragments. She swept past me without saying goodbye.

32

a all and as at bar barman certain drinks eyes flourish glasses his I in least mixed observed of people poured the there time twenty unbroken watching were wiped with years yet

42

I observed the barman as he wiped the as yet unbroken glasses and with a certain flourish poured and mixed drinks, all the time watching the people in the bar. There were at least twenty years of watching people in his eyes.

21

and bar black didn't don't drinks entered guys I in jackets know leather ordered remembered the they three were what who

25

The three guys in black leather jackets entered the bar and ordered drinks. I don't remember what they ordered. I didn't know who they were.

77

a about American another apprehensive are asked bar barman being beers black breaking but by capable covered divided do doing fidgeting glad glasses go hands he here himself his holding I'm immense in it it's john kept leather looking me my never not number occur of on one ordered perfection presence public quite round slightly so someone surface telephone that the their them then they they're those thought to underneath unhappy use watched were what would zippers

103

Those immense zippers divided the black leather surface that covered the American perfection underneath. Their hands were quite capable of breaking the glasses they were holding, but it would never occur to them to do so. The barman was unhappy about their being in his bar. He kept fidgeting about, looking slightly apprehensive. They ordered another round of beers. What are they doing in my bar, the barman asked himself. One by one, he watched them go to the john. Then he watched them use the public telephone. They're here to do a number on someone, he thought. I'm glad it's not me.

11

after barman before had left never said seen the them they

11

Never seen them before, said the barman, after they had left.

3

I leather replied

3

Leather, I replied.

4

agreed he leather yeah

4

Yeah, leather, he agreed.

34

a against apartment apartments bulwark city does have her imper-fection in intrusion is jacketed leather like many men my of on other particular said say she so subject the this three to what Whitehead

37

This is my apartment, she said to the three leather jacketed men. Her apartment, like so many other apartments, is a bulwark against the intrusion of imperfection. What does Whitehead have to say on this particular subject?

21

body contend has her imperfection it is lips long nose of she tall taste the thin to too walk with yet

39

Yet she has the imperfection of her nose to contend with. It is too long. The imperfection of her lips. Too thin. The imperfection of her body. Too tall. The imperfection of her walk, the imperfection of her taste.

28

all and are brown but couch doorman elevator everyone flaws friends her in jacketed leather men office on overlook prepared quite sitting so soft the these three to

35

But the elevator man, the doorman, everyone in her office, and all her friends are quite prepared to overlook these flaws. So are the three leather jacketed men sitting on the soft brown leather couch.

10

displeasing finds incongruity not of presence she slight the their

10

She finds the slight incongruity of their presence not displeasing.

29

and bedspread black bright enhance exotic floor foot four furniture gleaming her is jackets leather Mexican of perfection plant polished possessions silk she surface the their trousers wearing yellow

36

Their black leather jackets enhance the perfection of her possessions. The polished surface of her furniture, the Mexican bedspread, the exotic four foot plant, the gleaming floor, and the bright yellow silk trousers she is wearing.

39

a absorbed all and are blows bruised but can fabric faces from get hands have impassive is jackets knees leather longer look men need new no not of on reassurance resting the their they three tough trousers worn young

56

The three men are no longer young and their jackets are not new. They have a bruised look from the blows they have absorbed. But the leather is tough. The men have impassive tough faces, but their hands, resting on their knees, need all the reassurance they can get from the fabric of their worn jeans.

47

a also are available by chuck convey described descriptions discard doorman elevator every far farfetched from furniture have I it just kind loyalty man managed needs not now of office old on out people reliability so succession taxi taxis the their then they thrive to trips who

62

I have managed so far to convey the reliability and loyalty of the elevator man and the doorman. I have also described a succession of trips by taxi to and from the office. The descriptions are not farfetched. Taxis thrive on the needs of people, the kind of people who every now and then discard their old furniture, just chuck it out.

*a all and anything are array arrived bedroom been blank brain break-
fast by can change channels cigarette day design do face faces firm
fixed front fucked furniture had has her how I illuminated imprinted
in interiors it large left let's limits men mirror morning much newly of
on once one other out person pieces place remained room routine same
she smoked sound spotlight succession switch the there to tossed
treasured turn unchanged view voices was were with*

117

Everything I once treasured in her place has been tossed out. One day
men arrived with large pieces of furniture and in turn left with other
large pieces of furniture. The view from the front room remained the
same. There are, let's face it, limits to how much any one person
can change anything. She fixed her breakfast in a newly designed
kitchen, fucked in a newly designed bedroom, illuminated by a newly
designed array of spotlights. The morning routine remained unchanged. The face in the mirror remained blank. She smoked a cigarette. Imprinted on her brain were a succession of faces, interiors, and
the sound of voices. All she had to do was to switch channels.

29

*a ability and as available certain communicating did enabled express
having her invite meet men mind on she so speak the them three to
unspoken visit was what without*

34

Her ability to speak enabled her to meet the three men and without
having to express what was on her mind, invite them to visit her, communicating, as she did so, a certain availability.

53

*a afraid against all American Anadelle Anadelle's Arizona as at been
black book defense did dinky do face Georgina Glow guardian had
have head her in indignation jackets leather librarian like look looked
men not of on perfection read reminded she single the their then they
three to town was who women wore*

75

To the three men she looked like Anadelle the librarian in their dinky
town in Arizona. They had been afraid of her. They wore their black
jackets as a defense against women who reminded them of Anadelle
Georgina Glow, the head librarian. Anadelle was the guardian of
American perfection in their town. They did not have to read a single

book, all they had to do was to look at the indignation on Anadelle's
face . . .

9

a how know librarian resembled she that to was

10

How was she to know that she resembled a librarian?

105

*a an and any anything apartment avoided balanced being between
black blowing bought brain by cab city could cover crash did die
disharmonious distance doorman down drop either elevator embank-
ment emotion everything evoke fearful for furiously go good gray hail
have he hear her him his if imprinted in into investments it jackets
leather light man men might mind morning mumbled new not now objects of office on or overlapped painting pavement perfection plant
pleasant plunge rang realism resembled Rosenquist screwed see she
stare still stood suddenly taxi terror that the thought three to unaware
unpleasant waiting was well were whistle white would wrong York*

167

The objects in her apartment were either white or a light gray. In her
mind she could see the distance she now would have to cover between her apartment and her office. The thought did not evoke any
pleasant or unpleasant emotion. She rang for the elevator. The elevator
man avoided her stare. He mumbled good morning. He was fearful
that the three men were still in her apartment. She stood on the pavement waiting for the doorman to hail a cab. She could hear him blowing his whistle furiously. The realism of New York City was imprinted
on her brain. It overlapped the realism of being screwed by three men
in leather jackets. The overlapping was not disharmonious. If anything,
it resembled a painting by Rosenquist. A well balanced perfection of
terror. She was not unaware that anything might suddenly go wrong.
The elevator might plunge down, the taxi might crash into an em-
bankment, her investments might drop, and the plant she bought might
suddenly die.

66

*a adoration all also an and are be boss coat costume day discreet
downpour drink during expensive eyes familiar far filled forsaken god
had have her imagination in invited it lift lived loyal might of offer
on one only out place raincoat rained rampant ran secretary several
since she shoes smiled some sudden the them then those timidly to
unexpected up was way with wore would*

101

On the day it rained she wore her raincoat. It was an expensive coat. She had several. Her secretary was familiar with all of them. The secretary was also familiar with her shoes and her costumes. The secretary smiled timidly. She was discreet. She was loyal. Only her imagination ran rampant. One day, during one of those sudden and unexpected downpours, her boss would offer her a lift, and then, since she lived in some god forsaken far out of the way place, she might be invited up to have a drink . . . The eyes of the secretary are filled with adoration.

35

a Africa alphabetical bed book could fixed from had hair her lent likely low lying make more morning near not of on out reading recall she sitting someone table the title to was where why

56

She fixed her hair in the morning. From where she was sitting she could make out the title of a book lying on the low table near her bed. The title was *Alphabetical Africa*. She could not recall reading the book. Someone had lent it to her. More likely someone had forced it on her. Why????

103

a about again all although an and are around as bathroom be bedroom but by can cash casually closet couch dining doorman down drawers eighth evaluate examining expensive fear few floor foot for former four fridge from have her horse husbands if in inside is know leather leave like loyal men might mirrored monogrammed never no not nothing of office on one open opens or out park pass people permitted plant pull reluctant riders ridden room secretary see she squint stroll take that the them themselves there they thick three to towels tropical trying unfamiliar unimpeded view visit wall weekend will window would

171

The three men know nothing about her. They evaluate her by examining the four foot tropical plant, the expensive leather couch, the bedroom, and the dining room. They know nothing about the office, or her loyal secretary, or her former husbands, or the people she will visit on the weekend. All they can see is the mirrored wall in the bathroom, and the thick monogrammed towels. They casually open a few closets and pull out a few drawers, but there is no cash around. From the window they have an unimpeded view of the riders in the park. They know the park inside out, although they have never ridden a horse in the park. The view from the eighth floor is unfamiliar to them.

They squint, as if trying to see themselves down there. They would like to take a stroll in the park, but are reluctant to leave, not wishing to pass the doorman for fear that they might never be permitted in again. One of them opens the fridge . . .

164

a about absence absent acquaintance again all American among and any apartment appreciated are as at back barmen be bedroom bedspread been best between bread break bright buffet but by carefully carrying cheese cleaning clues cold color conspicious continuation crowd dainty definite discouraging displayed distance don't doorman's drinks elevator erased even evenings everyone's everything examined except firmly floor footprints for forth found freezer fridge friend furthermore glass gleaming greeting guests had hand have her holding home how hundred ice in inquisitive inside invited is it know lack least leather lips little maison man's matter may means men name neatly never no not nothing nourishment occurred of off offering on one other others outfit packed party pâté perhaps perplexed platters present pressing probably prowl reduce remembers scrutinized sealed searching settle sexual she silver so something soup spends splendidly table that the their there those three throws toast to tomato totally triangles twice two uniformed view waiters walking well what white who will write yearly yellow

307

They know nothing about her except what is on view. What is on view is splendidly displayed. It is, furthermore, on view in order to be appreciated. On the other hand, the interior of the fridge is discouraging. It is not packed. There is a definite lack of nourishment inside that gleaming combination freezer and fridge. They settle for tomato soup and cheese on white toast. What is not on view is the party she throws twice yearly. At least one hundred are invited. Again, everything on view is scrutinized. There are two barmen and two uniformed waiters offering the guests pâté on dainty triangles of white American bread. The pâté is *pâté maison*. It is nothing to write home about. The little triangles of bread are neatly arranged on silver platters. Nothing but the best. She remembers everyone's name and spends all evening walking back and forth in her bright yellow or orange outfit greeting friends. She believes the bright color will reduce the distance between her and the others, those inquisitive acquaintances who prowl the apartment searching for clues, searching for something, they probably don't even know what it is . . . perhaps it is what is absent, that what is not to be found among the crowd at the buffet table . . . all her guests holding ice cold drinks, but no one pressing the glass so firmly as to break it. No, that had never occurred . . . Perhaps her guests are perplexed by the absence of any conspicuous sexual clues. But the doorman's lips are sealed. The elevator man's lips are sealed as well. The three men in leather have lips that are by no means sealed, but they are not present. They are absent. Totally absent. No matter how carefully one may examine the bedroom floor, or the bedspread, their footprints have been erased by the cleaning woman.

17

American an and another diary great in introduction is my Saturday simply Sunday the this to weekend

20

This is an introduction to my diary. In the diary the Great American Weekend is simply another Saturday and Sunday.

47

a and apartment are carefully design doing escape expect fighter for George given going hatch he he's how I I'll interior is jet latest me mechanism my navy new now oh on returns said she see smile smiling splendid the to up weekend whose working yes you

55

I expect I'll see you on the weekend, she said to me.

Yes, George and I are going, I said carefully. Smiling.

She returns my smile. How is George?

He's splendid.

Whose apartment is he doing now?

Oh, he's given up interior design. He's working on a new escape hatch for a navy jet fighter.

8

did he I love my place to what

8

I love what he did to my place.

7

it let me must see sometime you

7

You must let me see it sometime.

9

at had I it party seen the thought you

9

I thought you had seen it at the party.

4

didn't invite me you

4

You didn't invite me.

11

an Brazil from I it next oversight return was when year

11

It was an oversight. Next year, when I return from Brazil.

25

*believe besides Brazil care couldn't do don't flatly George going he her
I in look miserable oh said she's slightest the to told why you*

34

She's going to Brazil, I told George.

Don't believe her, he said. Besides, why do you care.

Oh, I couldn't care in the slightest.

I don't believe you, he said flatly. You look miserable.

46

*ability about after along another are ask at Brazil car could despite do
drives George going have her independence no now one overtaking
parkway rear said same seat she sit table Taconic the this thrust to
two upon valises was we weekend what why will wishes*

66

Now she drives along the Taconic Parkway overtaking one car after another. Her two valises are on the rear seat. Despite her independence,
her ability to do what she wishes, this weekend has been thrust upon
her. She could have said no. She could have said she was going to
Brazil. We will sit at the same table. George will ask her about Brazil.
Why Brazil?

73

*against and any anyone as at available because bed been besides but
by case company desired doesn't dressed elegance else encounter even
event familiar flaunt had has have her herself if impeccably in independence invite men mitigated most needed next not of other ours
perfection perfumed perhaps pleasurable prefer represented room self-
assured she single skin sleep smooth something teeth the their these
they this to wanted was weekend were white will would young*

95

She has the next room to ours. As if to flaunt her independence she
doesn't invite anyone to her room. In any event most of the single
young men at this weekend prefer the company of other single young

men, but even if this were not the case, even if these self-assured impeccably dressed young men had been available, their elegance, their smooth perfumed skin, their white teeth would have mitigated against a pleasurable encounter in bed, perhaps because they represented the familiar perfection, and in bed something else besides perfection was wanted, needed, desired.

74

a after almost and any apart as aware awed back before below black brand by carpet closed couch did ever familiar fixtures found front furniture had half helpless her horsemen immobile in interests it jacketed kneeling knelt leather legs lighting men mind new not oblivious of on one other own paintings park perfection place pricks row sat seen she somewhat sucked surroundings the their them then they three took two view visit volition walls

127

Had any of the three black leather jacketed men ever seen her kneeling before? She did not mind kneeling in front of them. She did it of her own volition. She found the experience an interesting one. It took place in her familiar surroundings. On her own carpet. She knelt in front of them as they sat on her brand new leather couch, their legs apart, and sucked their pricks, one after the other, one then two then three. They sat back with half closed eyes, not oblivious of the perfection of her furniture, her lighting fixtures, the paintings on the walls, the view of the horsemen in the park below . . . they sat in a row, immobile, almost helpless, extremely aware and somewhat awed by their surroundings.

43

a all and back blouse but butter can carefully carried dinky drained emotion faint familiar flat from head hear her home I in it librarian men of recollection said she speaking succinctly that the their them three to town unbuttoning voice whatever while

59

I can hear her speaking to them. I can hear her familiar flat brittle voice, a voice that drained all emotion from whatever she said, a voice that carried to the three men the faint recollection of the head librarian in their dinky town back home. But whatever she said, she said it carefully, succinctly, while unbuttoning her blouse.

CROSSING THE GREAT VOID

PART ONE

On the map of the East Coast on which was printed DISCOVER AMERICA BY CAR, Zachary has marked the places, the points of interest, the State Parks, State Monuments, Memorials and Historic Sites he has visited together with his mother and uncle Umberto. He has also circled Atlantic City, Cape May, Newark, Peekskill, West Point, Ossining, Patchogue, and Orient Point.

He stares at the bald spot on the back of his uncle's head. They're on the Taconic State Parkway. Isn't it beautiful? says his mother as she looks straight ahead. Zachary doesn't know if she is addressing him or his uncle.

On a map of the United States, Zachary has circled the Mojave desert in southern California, the Gila desert in southern Arizona, the Black Rock desert in northwestern Nevada, and Death Valley in eastern California and southern Nevada, knowing that all these deserts must have something in common with the Great North African Desert where his father disappeared on a mission behind enemy lines in 1941.

Zachary stares at a blank piece of paper. As blank, he thinks, as the Great North African Desert on a map. Somewhere within that blankness stood his father, patiently waiting to be found.

Punctually at six his uncle Umberto comes to visit every Monday, Wednesday, and Friday. One long peal of the doorbell, and his mother races to the front door. She doesn't want to keep his uncle waiting a split second longer than necessary. The sound of her high heels against the waxed-wood floor frame in his mind a succession of shots that puncture his eardrums, that puncture the blank piece of paper in his hand, that puncture the blankness, the vast blankness of all the deserts in the world. When his uncle Umberto opens the door of Zachary's room, as usual without first knocking, Zachary is crouching on all fours, playing with his toy automobiles. They were a gift from his uncle. Each one is an exact replica of an American car. As his uncle silently observes Zachary, can he possibly fail to notice the small firecracker that has been attached to one of the cars, a black passenger car. That evening, after dinner, while his mother is doing the dishes, his uncle raises the subject: Isn't Zachary a bit too old to play with toy cars . . . and why does he attach a firecracker to one of the cars. I would like to know the meaning of that!

Zachary, why do you keep harping on deserts in every essay you write, his English teacher had wanted to know. For one thing, deserts are not quite as empty and blank as you seem to believe. For another, as metaphors, they leave a great deal to be desired.

Zachary and his mother share the same bathroom. In the medicine cabinet his mother has arranged, side by side, a jar of skin lotion, a jar of skin cleanser, a skin moisturizer, a bottle of shampoo, an antiperspirant roll, rouge, lipsticks, eyeshadow, mascara, hair lotion, scented talcum powder, eau de cologne, perfume, nail polish. The accoutrements of feminine perfection. The large adjustable safety razor on the second shelf doesn't belong to his mother. Neither does the bright green toothbrush. Of that, Zachary is convinced. The bristles of the toothbrush are damp on Tuesday, Thursday, and Saturday morning. They are not wet, Zachary discovered, but damp. Not wet wet but moist. Zachary saw his uncle's body for the first time at Cape May. He watched his uncle dive into the water. There was hair on his uncle's chest, on his shoulder blades, on the back of his neck, on his thighs and legs. How could his mother not be revolted by his uncle's body? His uncle laughed as soon as he realized that Zachary was afraid of the water. Zachary's mother was a good swimmer, but she pretended to be afraid, mimicking, it seemed to Zachary, his own fear. I will have to teach you, his uncle said to her, standing up to his waist in the water. Tiny beads of water clung to the thick growth of hair on his white corpulent body. Zachary walked away. The beach at Cape May was crowded with a great many men who resembled his uncle. At night Zachary was kept awake by a woman in the next room who monotonously repeated in a high-pitched voice, Please don't beat me, please don't beat me. But despite these words, the woman did not sound frightened. It occurred to Zachary that she might be repeating the same phrase over and over again because it pleased the man.

Where are we going today, Zachary asked his mother when his uncle drove up to their house in his brand new Cadillac. He had never seen her so excited before. Your uncle is taking us to the Desert Inn Restaurant in Hoboken.

I wish he had picked a restaurant with another name, said Zachary petulantly.

Oh Zach, said his mother, can't you ever drop the past?

Zachary takes the ferry to Staten Island and then a bus to the stadium where a team from Bensonhurst is playing soccer against a visiting team from Italy. He watches attentively as the Italians win, 28:7. The middle-aged woman at his side is waving an Italian flag. Turning to her he says: My father used to play soccer. But he's been listed as missing in North Africa since '41. You poor kid, says the woman. You poor kid. I know exactly how you must feel. It's a crying shame.

With his forearms resting on the metal railings of the overpass, Zachary focused his father's World War II binoculars on the black Cadillac. According to his mother, the binoculars had been a gift from Il Duce to his father. Briefly, he focused on the massive jaw of his uncle behind the steering wheel, then pressed the red buttons on the device that steered his remote-controlled toy car. With his hearing aid turned off he wouldn't be able to hear the explosion that would rip his uncle's car apart. At the very worst it might sound like the waves breaking at Cape May.

I don't care for the way the boy keeps looking at me, said his uncle.

That's because he has trouble hearing you, his mother replied. He's trying to read your lips.

Bullshit. He's not reading my lips, said his uncle. I don't like it. Tell him to stop it.

Your uncle doesn't like the way you stare at him.
But I don't.
I've seen you.
I wish he would knock before entering my room, said Zachary. Could you please ask him to knock in the future.

On Zachary's birthday his uncle said: It's about time the boy did something useful.
What do you have in mind, his mother asked, but his uncle didn't elaborate. Each year in January his uncle bought a new Cadillac. He drove to their place straight from the showroom. Beaming, he waited for their response. It's the most beautiful car you've ever owned, Zachary's mother said. She would always sit next to his uncle in the car, while he sat in the back.

Where shall we drive to this time, his uncle asked them.
What about Atlantic City, we haven't been there in ages, said his mother. Or how about Cape May. We had such fun in Cape May.
Would you like to own a car like this one some day, asked his uncle. Not particularly, he had replied. His uncle had just nodded. The following week Zachary started to work in a garage.

He spent an entire afternoon servicing a black Cadillac. Methodically he checked the oil, the transmission fluid, the air conditioning, the brakes, the windshield wipers, the radio, the air pressure in the tires, the cigarette lighter, the automatic windows. You are spending far too much time on that car, the manager said. What's the matter. Are you asleep?

Zachary's uncle closely examined the map of North Africa that was fixed to the wall above his bed. Isn't it time that you replaced it with something else?
What do you do, uncle?
What do you mean?
What kind of business are you in?
I'm in the management business, his uncle said angrily. I manage a

great many things. More things than you can imagine. Now, get rid of that map. Zachary didn't hear the door slam. He had turned off his hearing aid.

Tell me honestly, are you afraid of him, Zachary asks his mother.

Afraid of your uncle. She laughs. He was your father's best friend. It was he who brought back your father's second pair of binoculars, his medals, and the sand goggles he wore in the desert. It was he who saw your father and his orderly, Vicente, leave on the secret mission from which they never returned.

Why have we never met his family?

Your uncle's?

Yes . . .

His wife and I don't get along, she replies reluctantly. His wife has always resented that your father had been a captain and your uncle only a noncommissioned officer.

Zachary dialed his uncle's number. After two rings a woman answered. When he did not speak up, she said: If it is who I think it is, you bitch, drop dead.

Zachary folded the map of Africa and placed it on his desk. He also removed the binoculars, the medals, and the sand goggles from the narrow shelf above his desk. At ten his mother tapped lightly on his door. As usual she was wearing her black lace dressing gown. As always she sat down on the bed at his side, reached for his hand, and began to speak about his father. She described their first encounter, then their second encounter, then the third unexpected encounter at the railroad station in Bologna. She spoke of a subsequent meeting in Milan, then a meeting in the Italian Alps, and finally the elopement in Venice. Zachary had never been to any of those places. She described in detail the hotels where they had stayed, the cafes frequented by his father, the color of the Italian sky on a Wednesday in February, the paintings by Carpaccio, the gala night at the officer's club, the ornate design of the paving stones in the piazza where his father for the first time held her hand, and finally the Lybian desert where his father had interrogated the British prisoners. They used to compliment your father on his excellent English. He had a good Oxonion accent with just a touch of Liverpool to it.

Had he ever been to Liverpool, Zachary asked her.

Briefly. He came to England while I was staying with some friends in Liverpool. He didn't approve of them and wanted to take me away. He was a bit jealous, I think. She laughed. It's a long time ago. In a matter of a week he had picked up the Liverpool accent. When he said, fish and chips, he could have fooled any Englishman. That's why he volunteered for the mission.

Zachary never once doubted or questioned anything she said. She spoke in a quiet voice, a melodious gentle voice, until her uninterrupted stream of reminiscences pulled him into sleep. He was twenty-four and weighed one hundred-and-thirty-two pounds. He got along with the other mechanics at the garage, but refrained from mentioning that his father, Captain Benventucentino Zachary Malaparta Gruz, had been a member of the Italian Expeditionary Forces in North Africa, and that he was a distant relative of Mussolini's second cousin Fabrino Melchuz.

When last seen his father had worn the uniform of an English colonel in His Majesty's Royal Household Artillery, and his orderly, Vicente, had been wearing the uniform of a regimental Sergeant-major. They had driven off in a captured Land Rover. In the official document in which Zachary's father was listed as missing, the exact nature of his mission was omitted. It merely stated that Captain Benventucentino Zachary Malaparta Gruz had failed to return from a dangerous and delicate mission from behind the enemy lines. Somewhat abruptly Zachary's uncle had left the room when his mother read aloud the letter she had received from the Italian government in response to her inquiry as to her husband's whereabouts. From other former military sources she had heard how the entire battalion had stood at attention for five minutes in the broiling sun as a tribute to Zachary's father. Three months later, when the battalion's soccer team was defeated by the English guards at the British army prisoner-of-war camp, the loss was in part attributed to the absence of Zachary's father, who used to play center forward on the team.

When Zachary, at the age of eight, had experienced difficulty hearing his mother recount the same story over and over again, she had taken him to an ear specialist, who advised her to get him a hearing aid. Zachary wore his hearing aid in his right ear, which he kept turned to whoever happened to be speaking.

Why didn't you volunteer for the mission as well, he asked his uncle.

Because I'm not a bloody hero.

For years after the war a great many men in and out of uniform came to visit his mother, to pay their respects to the wife of their former fellow officer. Some left snapshots of themselves. On a few photographs in his mother's album his mother is standing next to a man in uniform, the man's hand resting affectionately on her waist. But on her night table there is only one photograph, the ornately framed photograph of his father taken on the steps of the Hotel Minerva in Siena. His father was wearing a military-looking coat with gold braid on his sleeve and chest. A small silver whistle dangled from a chain around his neck. The coat was a trifle too large. It reached far below his knees and the long sleeves allowed only the fingers to protrude. Why doesn't he wear his rank on his coat, he had once asked his mother. It isn't done in Italy, she had said. One never wears one's rank on a heavy winter coat. Why is he wearing a whistle at the end of his chain. To summon his orderly, Vicente. And why is he standing at attention in front of the hotel.

Because he is an officer, she replied.

You see, his mother said proudly after the man who had telephoned earlier in the day had left their apartment. We may be living in New York City, but Italy has not forgotten your father. The man who just left is an official in the Italian State Department. He flew to New York to urge me not to give up hope. Your father may be alive. A man resembling your dear father has recently been seen in an oasis in North Africa. More the man couldn't say. His lips are sealed.

Never, never forget that your father was a captain in the Italian Expeditionary Forces, Zachary's mother said the first day he went to work as an automobile mechanic. That evening, after dinner, his uncle mentioned that his father had often spoken of his admiration for the American assembly-line production of cars.

Bullshit, thought Zachary.

As Zachary was greasing his uncle's car, one of the mechanics walked up to him and said:

If that Mafioso is really your uncle, then what are you doing here, greasing his car?

What kind of funerals do Mafiosos receive, Zachary asked his mother.

Irritated she said: How should I know?

He refrained from asking his uncle.

PART TWO

At first Zachary had not paid any attention to Track, the young woman who had brought her 1964 VW bus to the garage for a tune-up. When he told her that the car would also need new shocks, brakes, a muffler, a starter, and an engine job, she simply laughed, as if delighted by the amount of work her car required. The week before she had returned from Tunisia. Somewhat pointedly, Zachary remarked that his father was listed as missing in Libya after the defeat of the Italian army. Yes, it's easy to get lost in Africa, she replied almost diffidently.

The map of North Africa was still hanging on the wall above his bed. Somewhere in that great North African desert his father had disappeared, vanished into thin air. Since you appear to be so intrigued by North Africa, you'll be interested to know that the map of Blitlu, an oasis in the center of the Great Desert, is tatooed on my back, Track said the next time she came by to pick up her car.

Your back?

She had taken him by complete surprise. He was dumbfounded. He was also unprepared for what was to follow that evening at her place. He had no prior experience, no knowledge upon which he could base an appropriate response when hours later, at her house, she unbuttoned her blouse and proceeded to take it off. With the lights off, it was too dark in her bedroom for him to see the map of Blitlu. In addition to your hearing aid you also seem to need glasses, she said matter-of-factly. He was convinced that her remark was devoid of malice. It was not an accusation, but merely a statement of fact.

Her room is pitch dark and his eyes are tightly shut, perhaps a double precaution as he listens to her descriptions of the desert, to the detailed descriptions of the barren plains, though the term is misleading, since on close inspection plants can be found. The perennials are inconspicuous, partly because they are so small, and partly because their leaves are either missing or greatly reduced. What else does she say? He has trouble keeping his hearing aid in place. He is not certain how he came to find himself in such a precarious position, naked, thrusting his body forward, this forcefulness on his part being encouraged by her, or at least he assumed as much from her soft cries, sounds he could not hear but deduced from the motion of her lips, his hearing aid, the one he plugged into his right ear, lying on the floor. All in all, it is safe to assume that this situation evolved out of some prior mutual understanding, something that either he or she may have said.

He is infatuated with her knowledge of the entire North African region. In Bendin, a coastal city with a small harbor and long stretches of fine beach, the people prefer to remain indoors on account of the sun and intense heat. They do not care to have their already dark skins turn darker. When compelled to go out during the day, the inhabitants go miles out of their way to stay in the shade. The beaches are used exclusively by the tourists. The people in Bendin show their contempt for the tourists by calling them Eechklus. Many of the tourists staying in Bendin are on their way to visit the site of the great battle between the British and the gallant outnumbered Italian troups. A small number of the tourists try to make it to Blitlu where dope is available in quantity at a bargain price. Most of them never make it to Blitlu. Their cars break down or they lose their way. Many people still seem to think that by undertaking an arduous journey they are also going to discover something about themselves they have never known. Zachary felt disinclined to tell Track that, as far as he was concerned, discovering anything entailed listening to what people had to say, and until a better hearing aid was perfected he did not have great expectations of discovering anything new about himself.

Track did not seem to mind that he was a mechanic. Not at all. One could endlessly explore your body, she said, after he had removed his shirt, eagerly almost, although it entailed his having to hold the hearing aid in one hand. All the same, a woman, a naked woman who had been halfway across the African continent, was welcome to explore his body. You shrink each time I touch you. Why are you so afraid of being touched.

He could recall every minute of their second encounter. Sitting across from Track in her apartment, straining his ears to hear what she was saying. They were speaking about the flora and fauna of the desert, the unremitting loneliness, not to mention the incredible heat during the day and the unexpected chill at night. In retrospect he could only surmise that it was their mutual interest in the desert that had brought them together.

What do you really like? Track asked him. He was nonplussed by her question, he was also profoundly unprepared for it . . . If only she had asked him what he loved. The list is an endless one. To begin with he loved his father, last seen driving into the Great Desert, wearing the uniform of an English officer, he also loved his beautiful mother as she sat each night at his bedside speaking of his father, he also loved the coastline on the map of North Africa, that undulating Northern-most line to the south of which the solitary figure of his missing father, standing somewhere in the vast emptiness of the Great Desert, kept beckoning to him. In that respect his day is replete with love and the expectation of a contentment that is yet to come.

Yet, despite all her talk of Blitlu, he could not locate the oasis on his map of North Africa or on any other map of North Africa in the map division at the 42nd Street public library. Did Blitlu exist. Had she really been there. Why Blitlu. She was the first woman he had met who had been to Africa. Late at night she drove him back to his place in her 1964 VW bus, driving competently, but with a certain unmistakable disdain for the drivers she narrowly missed.

It was to be the last time he saw her.

Are you thinking of going back to Blitlu, he asked.

Can I drop you here . . . I don't want to run into your uncle, she said.

My uncle . . . How do you know my uncle?

He's everybody's uncle, she said condescendingly.

When the black Cadillac driven by his uncle exploded on the center lane of the Cross Bronx Expressway at two-thirty-seven, Zachary thought of a giant wave that was about to break and come crashing down on the sand. In addition to his uncle's death there were three fatalities and seventeen injured, mostly from the flying glass. I'm sorry, Zachary said to the policeman who came to see him at the garage. You'll have to speak up, I can't hear a word you're saying.

In his will, his uncle left Zachary's mother some property in North Africa, although the will did not specify what sort of property it was. He left Zachary his automobile. Zachary settled for half the book value with the insurance company. I'd better have a look at that property in North Africa, he told his mother.

You killed him, didn't you? She said quietly.

My hearing aid is acting up again, Zachary said. I can't hear a word you're saying. The following day as he and his mother were leaving the house, he heard her say: Well, I guess now you'll know what a Mafioso funeral is like. The black coffin had the same gleam as the black Cadillac only seconds before it was blown to pieces. Zachary never expected to emerge alive from the funeral. The next day he went to a travel agency on Second Avenue and Tenth Street.

PART THREE

It stood to reason that something had to precede Zachary's arrival in Bendin. He was quite aware of it. He could hardly pretend that out of the clear blue he had found himself in Bendin. Accordingly, it also stood to reason that a certain amount of planning must have gone into this undertaking, including a certain amount of diligent reading about the varied desert terrain. For instance, what one should do if one is bitten by a snake in the desert (a not uncommon occurence), or what one should do if one happens to run out of food, and how to deal with the ticks, locusts (eat them), woodlice, false scorpions, and sandflies. In the authoritative study of the desert, *Crossing the Great Void* by Major General Klip D. Jars, an entire chapter was devoted to the hazards of the desert. Major General Jars, who had fought the Italians in North Africa and had briefly been held prisoner by them, also stated the little-known fact that the bite of a sandfly may be followed by nausea, fever and often result in an inflamed and hardened lesion. Other hazards not to be underestimated are the shifting sand dunes, some of which are three hundred feet high. Zachary wondered if the author of *Crossing the Great Void* had ever been interrogated by his father.

In the colorful illustrated brochure he had picked up at the travel agency, the weather along the coast of North Africa was described as being idyllic, a tourist's paradise, but, as he discovered, weather aside, it was a familiar world. Most of the roads were paved, and there were telephone poles at regular intervals along the highways. In the town the men who emerged somewhat stealthily from their whitewashed houses seemed to have the same needs people have elsewhere. They congregated in outdoor cafes and loudly discussed their sexual prowess. One could say that in meeting in this fashion they were fulfilling a need. In being able to sit on small crudely made chairs around a wood table and drink the strong black coffee they were also fulfilling a need everyone readily acknowledged and respected. Indeed, one might conclude that the entire town was built for no other purpose than to allow these encounters between men to take place. As for the women, if truly they exist, their needs were taken care of less conspicuously. As a stranger, an Eechklu, people were at first inclined, Zachary realized, to believe that he had different needs. That his needs had exotic American names, such as Zenith or Caterpillar Harvester. Traveling from the airport he took note of the landscape, the lush semitropical vegetation, the whitewashed houses with their closed shutters, the occasional mule cart on the road, the barefoot men wearing daggers in their belts, and, once in a while, a black Cadillac overtaking the slowly traveling bus. It was reassuring to discover that there were two pharmacies in Bendin. He entered the one nearest the hotel and inquired if they carried batteries for his hearing aid. Yes, said the pharmacist. He had a large supply of batteries and also carried snake toxin, condoms, hash, and sleeping pills. Zachary purchased a dozen batteries and a package of razor blades made in Tanzania. The blades, he later discovered, were rusty and the batteries quite dead.

When the car driven by his uncle exploded, his uncle was tossed thirty feet into the air. As a result the traffic on the Cross Bronx was tied up for three hours.

He had arrived in Bendin in a state of uncontrollable excitement that effaced the past, erased, above all, those tedious hours in the garage. For the first time he could peer into himself and see, so to speak, nothing that might make him feel uneasy. No photographs, no upholstered armchairs, no heavy drapes, no telephone calls late at night, no thick wall-to-wall rugs, no medicine cabinets, no automobiles being raised and lowered for inspection in the garage, and above all, no faces, absolutely no faces, except one that came and went without any prior warning—although he attempted to expunge it from his mind, eliminate all traces of it from his brain, but Track in all her nakedness kept embracing him, kept pressing his face, his long moody face with the hearing aid attached to his right ear, into her snow-white breasts, while her legs encircled his midriff and her fingers dug into the back of his neck as she exhorted him to love her, as she urged him to abandon his restraint, which she should have known was quite out of the question. He had never abandoned his restraint with a woman. He had abandoned almost everything else: his job, his mother, his buddies at the garage, his various uncles, his entire past. Some time he would blame his hearing aid for not letting him hear the words of warning, the words of caution he knew he must have received.

Overnight it must have rained heavily. The pavement was wet. A man carrying an open umbrella passed beneath his window. Basically, it is still the world to which he is accustomed. The people staying at the hotel stare at him, not even taking the trouble to disguise their curiosity. By now he has grown accustomed to it. It must be his appearance, his childlike hesitant smile. Frequently, on the street, a dark calloused hand is stretched out toward him, while the beggar's face seeks to replicate his own facial contortion, hovering between a timid beseeching smile and a look of anger.

At the time he met Track, his uncle's omnipresence had presented a problem that preoccupied him day and night. But not having a retentive mind he could no longer remember why. It had been annoying not to be able frequently to hear what passed between his uncle and his mother knowing, as he had, that what passed between them might have had some bearing upon his being in North Africa. He was in Bendin, on his way to the desert to claim some property his mother had inherited. Originally, when he had planned this very trip it had not occurred to him that it would also entail his taking possession of some property located in Blitlu, an oasis in or near the center of the great desert. None of the lawyers were able to tell him if the property was of any value . . . apparently only his uncle had known, and his uncle was dead.

Why are you all of a sudden so interested in Blitlu, Track had asked him the last time he had seen her. What possible meaning can that insignificant oasis have for you? He could only come up with a vague response. Most likely she suspected him of being evasive. He remembers stealthily touching her body, his touch, his exploratory touch was in the nature of an inquiry. He had always, after all, intuitively known what women were like. Moreover, that kind of information was passed on by his buddies in the garage—therefore, there were no untoward surprises. He was, so to speak, prepared.

At his prompting, Track had written on a piece of paper torn from her spiral notebook the direction he was to follow to reach Blitlu. He kept the piece of paper between the pages of *Crossing the Great Void*. Admittedly, she could have easily given him false directions. She could easily, out of a certain pique perhaps, have sent him to a different oasis, and he, knowing how things are in this world, would not have been overly surprised. But so far her directions had been correct, and he had every reason to believe that the paved road that led from Birsut to the center of the desert did in fact exist, and that therefore the dangers that must have confronted his father, the danger of losing one's way in the great desert, had by virtue of the road been eliminated.

At the airport in Bendin he was told that there was a direct flight to Birsut leaving in ten days. He bought a one-way ticket. He inquired at the ticket counter if he could have a map of Birsut. Will you take care of me? asked the clerk. Zachary handed him a dollar and received a hand-drawn map of the town. A hotel, a pharmacy, a monument to pilots of the RAF, and the local market were marked on the map. He wondered if the pharmacy stocked fresh batteries for his hearing aid. From Birsut, he was told, it was only nineteen hours by car to Blitlu.

The flight to Birsut in the old former British airforce transport plane took seven hours. The plane landed at Birsut at three in the afternoon. Why is it, Zachary asked himself, that I can always see my face as others see it. I can see myself to the slight amusement of my fellow passengers gaping at the view of Birsut below. As they came in for the landing he could see the road, presumably the one he would take to Blitlu, splitting the desert into two equal halves. The airfield is crowded with junked planes from World War II, some with their wings missing, others minus engine and propellers. Upon closer examination, Zachary could see that all the planes had recently received a fresh coat of paint. If one did not examine them too closely, one might come away with the impression that this was a busy terminal. According to his map the town itself was only four miles from the airfield. Slowly he walked to the huge aluminum shed that served as the terminal.

He is the last passenger to leave the plane. There's no one waiting for him. He has to collect his thoughts. As he walks to the huge shed carrying his suitcase, he can feel the desert beckon to him. The broad diagonal stripes of pink and green that cover the entire shed do not strike him as incongruous. Elsewhere they might have been startling, but here, in the middle of nowhere, they seemed quite appropriate. He is not put out by the intense heat and is immune to the earsplitting sound of a single-engine plane near the entrance to the shed revving its engine prior to take off.

Are you going to take care of me? shouts the taxi driver. Sure, says Zachary, reaching for his wallet. Just take me to the hotel. Which hotel. Is there more than one? Zachary is having increasing trouble hearing what people say. He is on his last battery. As they drive through Birsut, he realizes that the town is larger than he has been led to expect. They pass an outdoor market, a cemetery, a leper hospital, a school, a large square with a fountain in the center, a barbershop, a garage. The doorman standing on the front steps of the Hotel de Barcelona salutes as he steps out of the taxi. He is an elderly man with a somewhat straggly mustache. Despite the heat he is wearing what appears to be an old military coat. From around his neck dangles a whistle. He carries Zachary's suitcase into the hotel lobby. Zachary's hearing aid has gone completely dead, and he cannot understand what the man is saying. He presses a coin into the man's hand, realizing that from now on he will have to rely on sign language until he is able to buy fresh batteries for his set. At the pharmacy, when he shows the pharmacist one of his dead batteries, the man shakes his head and then writes on a pad the single word, Blitlu. It is amazing, thinks Zachary, that they would carry batteries in Blitlu. Would his hearing be restored in Blitlu? From his room on the second floor he can see the desert. Blitlu beckons to him. Three days later he leaves for Blitlu. One day in Birsut is very much like the next. On an old army map dating back to 1940 he located Blitlu. On the map which was hanging from a wall in the lobby, the oasis was designated as a munition dump.

The hotel lobby was deserted when he left at five in the morning. Having smiled broadly at him and then saluted, the doorman blew his whistle, but Zachary could not hear the shrill sound that alerted the taxi driver who was to drive him to Blitlu. Thanks, said Zachary, pressing a coin into the outstretched hand.

Now he is bound for the center of the desert, and every step he is taking is bringing him closer to the center, and every step he has taken in the past has led to his being here. Even before he was aware of the center's existence, he was traveling towards it. Everything he has encountered so far appears familiar, as if at some time in the past his mother must have described it to him as she spoke of his father in the Italian Expeditionary Forces crisscrossing the desert. Consequently he feels convinced that what lies ahead will also prove to be familiar. After all, the emptiness he expects to encounter at the center will be no different from the emptiness he might experience in the interior of his room after it had been denuded of all his possessions, stripped of all the things he had clung to with such persistence, such tenacity, such great effort, as if his entire life depended on it.

New Directions Paperbooks

Walter Abish, *Alphabetical Africa*. NDP375.
In the Future Perfect. NDP440.
Minds Meet. NDP387.
Ilangô Adigal, *Shilappadikaram*. NDP162.
Alain, *The Gods*. NDP382.
David Antin. *Talking at the Boundaries*. NDP388.
G. Apollinaire, *Selected Writings*.† NDP310.
Djuna Barnes, *Nightwood*. NDP98.
Charles Baudelaire, *Flowers of Evil*.† NDP71.
Paris Spleen. NDP294.
Martin Bax. *The Hospital Ship*. NDP402.
Gottfried Benn, *Primal Vision*.† NDP322.
Jorge Luis Borges, *Labyrinths*. NDP186.
Jean-François Bory, *Once Again*. NDP256.
Kay Boyle, *Thirty Stores*. NDP62.
E. Brock, *The Blocked Heart*. NDP399.
Here. Now. Always. NDP429.
Invisibility Is The Art of Survival. NDP342.
Paroxisms. NDP385.
The Portraits & The Poses. NDP360.
Buddha, *The Dhammapada*. NDP188.
Frederick Busch, *Domestic Particulars*. NDP413.
Manual Labor. NDP376.
Ernesto Cardenal, *Apocalypse & Other Poems*. NDP441.
In Cuba. NDP377.
Hayden Carruth, *For You*. NDP298.
From Snow and Rock, from Chaos. NDP349.
Louis-Ferdinand Céline,
Death on the Installment Plan. NDP330.
Guignol's Band. NDP278.
Journey to the End of the Night. NDP84.
Stephen Clissold, *The Wisdom of the Spanish Mystics*. NDP442.
Jean Cocteau, *The Holy Terrors*. NDP212.
The Infernal Machine. NDP235.
M. Cohen, *Monday Rhetoric*. NDP352.
Cid Corman, *Livingdying*. NDP289.
Sun Rock Man. NDP318.
Gregory Corso, *Elegiac Feelings American*. NDP299.
Happy Birthday of Death. NDP86.
Long Live Man. NDP127.
Kenneth Cragg, *Wisdom of the Sufis*. NDP424.
Edward Dahlberg, *Reader*. NDP246.
Because I Was Flesh. NDP227.
David Daiches, *Virginia Woolf*. NDP96.
Osamu Dazai, *The Setting Sun*. NDP258.
No Longer Human. NDP357.
Coleman Dowell, *Mrs. October . . .* NDP368.
Robert Duncan, *Bending the Bow*. NDP255.
The Opening of the Field. NDP356.
Roots and Branches. NDP275.
Richard Eberhart, *Selected Poems*. NDP198.
Russell Edson. *The Falling Sickness*. NDP 389.
The Very Thing That Happens. NDP137.
Paul Eluard, *Uninterrupted Poetry*. NDP392.
Wm. Empson, *7 Types of Ambiguity*. NDP204.
Some Versions of Pastoral. NDP92.
Wm. Everson, *Man-Fate*. NDP369.
The Residual Years. NDP263.
Lawrence Ferlinghetti, *Her*. NDP88.
Back Roads to Far Places. NDP312.
A Coney Island of the Mind. NDP74.
The Mexican Night. NDP300.
Open Eye, Open Heart. NDP361.
Routines. NDP187.
The Secret Meaning of Things. NDP268.
Starting from San Francisco. NDP 220.
Tyrannus Nix?. NDP288.
Who Are We Now? NDP425.
Ronald Firbank, *Two Novels*. NDP128.
Dudley Fitts,
Poems from the Greek Anthology. NDP60.
F. Scott Fitzgerald, *The Crack-up*. NDP54.
Robert Fitzgerald, *Spring Shade*. NDP311.
Gustave Flaubert,
The Dictionary of Accepted Ideas. NDP230.
M. K. Gandhi, *Gandhi on Non-Violence*.
(ed. Thomas Merton) NDP197.
André Gide, *Dostoevsky*. NDP100.
Goethe, *Faust*, Part I.
(MacIntyre translation) NDP70.
Albert J. Guerard, *Thomas Hardy*. NDP185.

Henry Hatfield, *Goethe*. NDP136.
John Hawkes, *The Beetle Leg*. NDP239.
The Blood Oranges. NDP338.
The Cannibal. NDP123.
Death, Sleep & The Traveler. NDP393.
The Innocent Party. NDP238.
John Hawkes Symposium. NDP446.
The Lime Twig. NDP95.
Lunar Landscapes. NDP274.
The Owl. NDP443.
Second Skin. NDP146.
Travesty. NDP430.
A. Hayes, *A Wreath of Christmas Poems*. NDP347.
H.D., *Helen in Egypt*. NDP380
Hermetic Definition NDP343.
Trilogy. NDP362.
Robert E. Helbling, *Heinrich von Kleist*, NDP390.
Hermann Hesse, *Siddhartha*. NDP65.
C. Isherwood, *The Berlin Stories*. NDP134.
Lions and Shadows. NDP435.
Philippe Jaccottet, *Seedtime*. NDP428.
Gustav Janouch,
Conversations With Kafka. NDP313.
Alfred Jarry, *The Supermale*. NDP426.
Ubu Roi, NDP105.
Robinson Jeffers, *Cawdor and Medea*. NDP293.
James Joyce, *Stephen Hero*. NDP133.
James Joyce/Finnegans Wake. NDP331.
Franz Kafka, *Amerika*. NDP117.
Bob Kaufman,
Solitudes Crowded with Loneliness. NDP199.
Hugh Kenner, *Wyndham Lewis*. NDP167.
Kenyon Critics, *Gerard Manley Hopkins*. NDP355.
P. Lal, *Great Sanskrit Plays*. NDP142.
Tommaso Landolfi,
Gogol's Wife and Other Stories. NDP155.
Lautréamont, *Maldoror*. NDP207.
Irving Layton, *Selected Poems*. NDP431.
Denise Levertov, *Footprints*. NDP344.
The Freeing of the Dust. NDP401.
The Jacob's Ladder. NDP112.
O Taste and See. NDP149.
The Poet in the World. NDP363.
Relearning the Alphabet. NDP290.
The Sorrow Dance. NDP222.
To Stay Alive. NDP325.
With Eyes at the Back of Our Heads. NDP229.
Harry Levin, *James Joyce*. NDP87.
Garcia Lorca, *Five Plays*. NDP232.
Selected Poems.† NDP114.
Three Tragedies. NDP52.
Michael McClure, *Gorf*. NDP416.
Jaguar Skies. NDP400.
September Blackberries. NDP370.
Carson McCullers, *The Member of the Wedding*. (Playscript) NDP153.
Thomas Merton, *Asian Journal*. NDP394.
Gandhi on Non-Violence. NDP197.
The Geography of Lograire. NDP283.
My Argument with the Gestapo. NDP403.
New Seeds of Contemplation. NDP337.
Raids on the Unspeakable. NDP213.
Selected Poems. NDP85.
The Way of Chuang Tzu. NDP276.
The Wisdom of the Desert. NDP295.
Zen and the Birds of Appetite. NDP261.
Henri Michaux, *Selected Writings*.† NDP264.
Henry Miller, *The Air-Conditioned Nightmare*. NDP302.
Big Sur & The Oranges of Hieronymus Bosch. NDP161.
The Books in My Life. NDP280.
The Colossus of Maroussi. NDP75.
The Cosmological Eye. NDP109.
Henry Miller on Writing. NDP151.
The Henry Miller Reader. NDP269.
Remember to Remember. NDP111.
The Smile at the Foot of the Ladder. NDP386.
Stand Still Like the Hummingbird. NDP236.
The Time of the Assassins. NDP115.
The Wisdom of the Heart. NDP94.
Y. Mishima, *Confessions of a Mask*. NDP253.
Death in Midsummer. NDP215.

Eugenio Montale, *New Poems*. NDP410.
  Selected Poems.† NDP193.
Vladimir Nabokov, *Nikolai Gogol*. NDP78.
  The Real Life of Sebastian Knight. NDP432.
P. Neruda, *The Captain's Verses*.† NDP345.
  Residence on Earth.† NDP340.
New Directions in Prose & Poetry (Anthology).
  Available from #17 forward. #35, Fall 1977.
Robert Nichols, *Arrival*. NDP437.
Charles Olson, *Selected Writings*. NDP231.
Toby Olson, *The Life of Jesus*. NDP417.
George Oppen, *Collected Poems*. NDP418.
Wilfred Owen, *Collected Poems*. NDP210.
Nicanor Parra, *Emergency Poems*.† NDP333.
  Poems and Antipoems.† NDP242.
G. Parrinder, *Wisdom of the Early Buddhists*.
  NDP444.
  Wisdom of the Forest. NDP414.
Boris Pasternak, *Safe Conduct*. NDP77.
Kenneth Patchen, *Aflame and Afun of
    Walking Faces*. NDP292.
  Because It Is. NDP83.
  But Even So. NDP265.
  Collected Poems. NDP284.
  Doubleheader. NDP211.
  Hallelujah Anyway. NDP219.
  In Quest of Candlelighters. NDP334.
  The Journal of Albion Moonlight. NDP99.
  Memoirs of a Shy Pornographer. NDP205.
  Selected Poems. NDP160.
  Sleepers Awake. NDP286.
  Wonderings. NDP320.
Octavio Paz, *Configurations*.† NDP303.
  Eagle or Sun? NDP422.
  Early Poems.† NDP354.
Plays for a New Theater. (Anth.) NDP216.
J. A. Porter, *Eelgrass*. NDP438.
Ezra Pound, *ABC of Reading*. NDP89.
  Classic Noh Theatre of Japan. NDP79.
  Confucius. NDP285.
  Confucius to Cummings. (Anth.) NDP126.
  Gaudier-Brzeska. NDP372.
  Guide to Kulchur. NDP257.
  Literary Essays. NDP250.
  Love Poems of Ancient Egypt. NDP178.
  Pavannes and Divagations. NDP397.
  Pound/Joyce. NDP296.
  Selected Cantos. NDP304.
  Selected Letters 1907-1941. NDP317.
  Selected Poems. NDP66.
  Selected Prose 1909-1965. NDP396.
  The Spirit of Romance. NDP266.
  Translations.† (Enlarged Edition) NDP145.
Omar Pound, *Arabic & Persian Poems*. NDP305.
James Purdy, *Children Is All*. NDP327.
Raymond Queneau, *The Bark Tree*. NDP314.
  The Flight of Icarus. NDP358.
  The Sunday of Life. NDP433.
Mary de Rachewiltz, *Ezra Pound:
  Father and Teacher*. NDP405.
M. Randall, *Part of the Solution*. NDP350.
John Crowe Ransom, *Beating the Bushes*.
  NDP324.
Raja Rao, *Kanthapura*. NDP224.
Herbert Read, *The Green Child*. NDP208.
P. Reverdy, *Selected Poems*.† NDP346.
Kenneth Rexroth, *Assays*. NDP113.
  Beyond the Mountains. NDP384.
  Bird in the Bush. NDP80.
  Collected Longer Poems. NDP309.
  Collected Shorter Poems. NDP243.
  Love and the Turning Year. NDP308.
  New Poems NDP383.
  One Hundred More Poems from the Japanese.
    NDP420.
  100 Poems from the Chinese. NDP192.
  100 Poems from the Japanese.† NDP147.
Rainer Maria Rilke, *Poems from
    The Book of Hours*. NDP408.
  Possibility of Being. NDP436.
Arthur Rimbaud, *Illuminations*.† NDP56.
  Season in Hell & Drunken Boat.† NDP97.
Edouard Roditi, *Delights of Turkey*. NDP445.

Selden Rodman, *Tongues of Fallen Angels*.
  NDP373.
Jerome Rothenberg, *Poems for the Game
    of Silence*. NDP406.
  Poland/1931. NDP379.
Saikaku Ihara, *The Life of an Amorous
    Woman*. NDP270.
St. John of the Cross, *Poems*.† NDP341.
Jean-Paul Sartre, *Baudelaire*. NDP233.
  Nausea. NDP82.
  The Wall (Intimacy). NDP272.
I. Schloegl, *Wisdow of the Zen Masters*. NDP415.
Delmore Schwartz, *Selected Poems*. NDP241.
Stevie Smith, *Selected Poems*. NDP159.
Gary Snyder, *The Back Country*. NDP249.
  Earth House Hold. NDP267.
  Regarding Wave. NDP306.
  Turtle Island. NDP381.
Gilbert Sorrentino, *Splendide-Hôtel*. NDP364.
Enid Starkie, *Arthur Rimbaud*. NDP254.
Stendhal, *Lucien Leuwen*.
  Book II: *The Telegraph*. NDP108.
Jules Supervielle, *Selected Writings*.† NDP209.
W. Sutton, *American Free Verse*. NDP351.
Nathaniel Tarn, *Lyrics . . . Bride of God*. NDP391.
Dylan Thomas, *Adventures in the Skin Trade*.
  NDP183.
  A Child's Christmas in Wales. NDP181.
  Collected Poems 1934-1952. NDP316.
  The Doctor and the Devils. NDP297.
  Portrait of the Artist as a Young Dog.
    NDP51.
  Quite Early One Morning. NDP90.
  Under Milk Wood. NDP73.
Lionel Trilling, *E. M. Forster*. NDP189.
Martin Turnell, *Art of French Fiction*. NDP251.
  Baudelaire. NDP336.
Alan Unterman. *The Wisdom of the Jewish
    Mystics*. NDP423.
Paul Valéry, *Selected Writings*.† NDP184.
P. Van Ostaijen, *Feasts of Fear & Agony*.
  NDP411.
Elio Vittorini, *A Vittorini Omnibus*. NDP366.
  Women of Messina. NDP365.
Linda W. Wagner. *Interviews with William
    Carlos Williams*. NDP421.
Vernon Watkins, *Selected Poems*. NDP221.
Nathanael West, *Miss Lonelyhearts &
    Day of the Locust*. NDP125.
G. F. Whicher, tr., *The Goliard Poets*.† NDP206.
J. Williams, *An Ear in Bartram's Tree*. NDP335.
Tennessee Williams, *Camino Real*. NDP301.
  Cat on a Hot Tin Roof. NDP398.
  Dragon Country. NDP287.
  Eight Mortal Ladies Possessed. NDP374.
  The Glass Menagerie. NDP218.
  Hard Candy. NDP225.
  In the Winter of Cities. NDP154.
  One Arm & Other Stories. NDP237.
  Out Cry. NDP367.
  The Roman Spring of Mrs. Stone. NDP271.
  Small Craft Warnings. NDP348.
  Sweet Bird of Youth. NDP409.
  27 Wagons Full of Cotton. NDP217.
William Carlos Williams,
  The Autobiography. NDP223.
  The Build-up. NDP259.
  Embodiment of Knowledge. NDP434.
  The Farmers' Daughters. NDP106.
  Imaginations. NDP329.
  In the American Grain. NDP53.
  In the Money. NDP240.
  Many Loves. NDP191.
  Paterson. Complete. NDP152.
  Pictures from Brueghel. NDP118.
  The Selected Essays. NDP273.
  Selected Poems. NDP131.
  A Voyage to Pagany. NDP307.
  White Mule. NDP226.
  W. C. Williams Reader. NDP282.
Yvor Winters, *E. A. Robinson*. NDP326.

**Complete descriptive catalog available free on request from
New Directions, 333 Sixth Avenue, New York 10014.**   † Bilingual